Funkle Fattie

Funkle Fattie is dedicated to Lucy, my version of Gramps. This story is for all the outsiders. I salute the Funkle in you. For Karen, Shannon, Pat and Alisa who helped inspire every word in this book. And for Katie, my favorite person and fellow writer, I thank you.

PROLOGUE

A nurse enters a visibly posh medical office. She hands the doctor --a curious, red-headed man who looks to be about fifty and is buried in a case -- a stack of folders. He sits comfortably in a very expensive high-backed leather cushioned chair. His desk is scattered with patients' folders, conspicuously color-coded and numbered, that rub against framed photos that decorate his desk.

The nurse is a lovely, middle-aged woman who wears pink scrubs that hug her low-riding breasts which unfortunately meet her protruding gut. She stands at the entrance to the office. She has strawberry blonde hair and uneven skin with one big bump on the fold of her mouth. It is the kind of bump that should be a mole but has no clear color. It's simply a pinkish, unsightly bump. So the bumpy lady interrupts politely in a pleasant voice --- one that doesn't really match the mole --- and breaks the doctor's busy work.

She interrupts, "Sir, you asked me to let you know when the jazz series at the park begins."

The doctor pays attention now, "Yes."

She continues, "I have the flyer with the schedule. It came yesterday. Shall I leave it on your desk?"

He affirms, "Yes."

She turns to exit but then remembers, "Oh, and your schedule at the hospital has changed for next week so I may have to move some of our patients' appointments. But I will certainly let you know."

He smiles again in agreement, "Perfect. And please ask

Angela to restock the lollipops. We are dangerously low," he laughs, his dentist bleached veneers peaking out.

She scratches her pink bump as she speaks, "You got it, wouldn't want to have a lollipop emergency."

Upon leaving his office, she laughs at her own witty repartee.

The doctor ruffles through the jazz series flyer, He suddenly finds himself lost in thought. Triggered by the photo of the jazz impresario on the cover, he grazes his palm over the glossy flyer. Soon he is transported back many years. He remembers the sound of the saxophone and the web of lies that permanently changed his whole world one fateful summer.

This is the tale of Funkle Fattie.

Chapter One

There are certain people from your childhood who, no matter how hard you wish you could wish away, you will never forget. These people are linked to the important memories, the ones that are indelibly etched deep in the caverns of your brain, the ones that no matter how hard you resist or deny, make you who you are. Every decision, every choice you make is somehow influenced by these memories. Peter Funkle, or should I say, the legend of Funkle Fattie is etched in the caverns of my brain still, all of these thirty years later.

My name is Tom Greene. Many years ago, I was known as Greeney, the bad kid from the wrong side of the tracks. This is my memoir of the tale or what some call the urban legend of Funkle Fattie.

It was late summer, 1974. As I stood cowering like a baby near the edge of Salter's Pond on this beautiful day in Massachusetts, the sounds of the Seagulls seemed to me, vultures now. The sounds of kids playing seemed to me, screams now. I remember watching as if all the events took place in slow motion. When I recall that day, I can still hear Jim Croce's, "Bad, Bad Leroy Brown" playing on one of our portable radios. For the most part the music was mostly drowned out by the sounds of violence. I still wince when I hear that song today.

I couldn't make myself small enough or inconspicuous enough especially with my give-away red mane. The ends of my fingers and toes tingled from the nervous adrenaline that flowed through my tiny body. My heart pounded out of my chest. I was witnessing the most horrific event of my boyhood. I knew it then but I could do nothing to stop it at the time. I didn't mean for it to happen, but somehow I knew I had caused it. My cluttered brain could not comprehend all that I had set up which was now crumbling before me like a badly made cake.

If you had been a passer-by at the pond that day, maybe you would've only seen boys rough-housing. And maybe you would have walked by thinking, "Oh boys will be boys." But upon closer inspection, nothing was farther from the truth. Nothing else mattered, not even the subsequent whys or should-haves or what-ifs, just the stark, gritty truth. And I knew all too well, what it was.

Peter Funkle -- otherwise known as Skunka-Funka or Funkle Fattie or Chunkle-Funkle -- and I refer to him as Pete or any of the aforementioned -- was getting the life pounded out of him by four thugs who I was too yellow to admit were not half as cool as they claimed. It's weird how the system is set up. It's like Roulette. Maybe at another school I would have been fire-crotch or Bozo or Howdy Doody, the outcast. Funkle would have been the cool, fat, super-sized lug of a funny guy. But it just didn't work out that way. It's all a massive set-up, really. The tough kids, who by the way are usually ugly with no brains and very few teeth, choose the weak link and it's all over. It just is -- Roulette for the junior circuit. It's sort of a massive preparation for corporate America.

So on this day when my boyhood took a very dark turn, four guys all rotated getting their kicks and punches in as Funkle gripped his muddy stick tightly. He put up a good, tough front as if he had a chance against Kenny, Waldo or any these guys.

Waldo...now he was a real sight for sore eyes. Waldo was this kid with three teeth jutting out of the same spot on his top gum. He also had one gray strand of hair - -a birth-defect -- adorning his messy Mick Jagger-like mop. He smoked Camels with no filters out of the side of his chapped, bumble-bee stung lips. We never talked about or dared to bring up the fact that he was fifteen years old. The idiot had been held back several grades. It was a sore subject. Waldo, incidentally, had been with more than ten girls by that point or at least the ones we knew of! And he had gone all the way. I mean that was power in the sixth and seventh grade, teeth or no teeth. The girls flocked to him.

It is so obvious that school, as it is designed, is a massive set-up really, pre-determined by a multitude of factors including looks, status and sexual prowess but never by brains. Waldo was ugly and in fact, a total jerk, but it had been somehow determined by some random someone that he was cool, a catch. And so it was. It had been ordained as truth.

Waldo kicked Funkle in his dimpled, jelly belly. He aimed hard and laser-straight with his steel-toe boots as he hollered curse words and hurled insults. He rarely missed. It went like this. Kick! *moan* Kick! *moan* Kick! *squeal*

I wasn't even the one being beaten and I was ready to puke

"Funkle, you sissy, you smelly, skanky, shit-bag," Waldo wailed.

I hid behind the other guys, "Yeah, yeah. Now grab it Waldo. Take it."

Truth: I was petrified. What a coward I was... still am.

Funkle was edging closer and closer to the rock formation at the edge of the pond. When Kenny kicked the muddy stick out of Funkle's hand, Pete became distracted by a thought. Suddenly events were set in motion. It seemed to me that it just happened so fast. At the same time it felt like it lasted for hours.

One single tear ran down my face. I don't know where it came from since I felt like all the liquid in my body had been turned to ice-cold stone. My heart pounded so hard out of my chest, it threatened to break through the skin and explode.

By universal consensus, I was a coward. There is no need for me now to wonder had I or could I have? I was a coward and by definition -- since I can never take back that moment -- I am a coward. It is part of the many facets of who I chose to be. I accept that branding. But I will work the rest of my life to live it down.

The definition of Coward n.: Watching the demise of a legend named Funkle Fattie. Doing nothing. Freezing. Having coolant replace blood in your veins. Being dead frozen when you are called upon to act. Doing nothing. Used in a sentence: I let fear supersede any ounce of moral code I owned and by making that choice, I am a coward.

Kenny screamed back at me to come with...

Kenny...now there is a guy I will never forget. I think he went on to become an actor. He looked like James Dean except he had really dark freckles over his alabaster skin and a huge Adam's apple. But he had the same handsome bone structure, countenance and swagger of Dean. He knew he was cool too. The girls loved him too and in this case it wouldn't have mattered what school he attended, he would have always been the hot guy.

So Kenny warned as he yelped, "Tommy, ditch, man. Ditch! Go!"

All I could think was, "What had we done? Oh Lord, what had we done? What would I tell my grandfather? What would become of us?"

Truth told, I thought of my own fate more than Pete's.

Chapter Two

The First Day of School 1973...

It was dark and damp on this Fall morning in Ipswich, Massachusetts, September of 1973. The air was so crisp it made me cantor a bit. Partly this enthusiasm was due to the chill and partly due to the anticipation of the new season. I actually always loved the first day of school. I remember this day specifically the way you do the most inane memories, because my blue and burgundy rugby shirt had a damp feel to it and it kept sticking to my skin. Also, I kept looking down (as I made the half-mile trek to school) to see if I could see the reflectors on my sneakers. I could.

Later that morning Mrs. Boone puttered around with Kenny, Waldo and I close at her heels. I have to admit she was quite a sexy number. She always wore little wrap dresses which allowed her perky breasts to hang in a hammock-like hold for dear life. She never wore a bra either so if she leaned over just enough...oh man, or at least we had hoped! Sometimes her long blonde hair would separate and fall right over her breasts. To me she was the perfect combination of Peggy Lipton from "Mod Squad" -- my favorite show -- and Mrs. Brady! Wholesome, sexy and a gun-wielding bad-ass all in one package! Aah, young love! It was great fun to witness boobs that dared to pop out and say, "hi." As a 12 year-old boy, I was so easily stimulated.

That morning, I remember all the kids scurrying to and from the coat-room as yet more children arrived later, entering the class during the bell. All the late-comers were putting their gear into the coat-room, getting situated while Mrs. Boone tried to distract Peter Funkle or Pete as he was known to the nice kids in the class.

While Pete stayed distracted, Kenny, Waldo and I helped Mrs. Boone prepare a birthday cake for his birthday. Kenny put the candles on the cake while I prepared a lunch tray that included a paper plate, a pint of milk, and a birthday card from the class.

Finally Waldo filed out carrying the cake...

"Happy Birthday to you," the class warbled out of tune.

Kenny and I remained in the coat-room. Sneakily, I added Ex-Lax into the milk on Peter's tray. We laughed and headed out with the prepared tray as we joined in the singing.

Why boys find bodily excrement and the sounds of gas that precede bodily excrement, so fulfilling, is still a mystery to me, but it remains true. Farts are golden, the pinnacle, when you're twelve. Shit is even better.

Waldo held the cake in front of Peter, now sitting at his desk.

"Make a wish Funkle," I hollered. Kenny set the tray in front of him.

"Happy Birthday, Peter," Mrs. Boone naively chirped.

Funkle wished hard and blew out the candles. He was a pretty cute kid in retrospect. Although. It has taken me many years to see him from that point of view. I think it happened after the birth of my own son. Compassion really takes on a new meaning when you join the ranks of parenthood.

Waldo cooperated fully, "May I cut him a piece, Mrs. Boone?"

"Oh that would be lovely Waldo, thank you," she answered.

The other boys, in on the prank, snickered.

Mrs. Boone flinched, "Careful. OK I'll serve the rest of you. Take a seat everyone. C'mon, c'mon. Sit, Sit."

"Read the card, Peter!" I gloated.

One of the boys made a loud fart sound by smacking his lips on his hands. Peter looked up but tried to ignore it.

"Thanks Mrs. Boone," Peter swooned.

"Oompa Loompa, doopity doo..." Kenny teased.

"Stop that right now Kenny," Mrs. Boone demanded.

"Yes, ma'am," Kenny complied.

The razzing wasn't lost on Pete. He just chose to ignore it. What a gift is choice. He opened up his card and smiled half way. Everyone waited while Mrs. Boone served slices of the cake. I think she made it herself. Perfect as with everything she did, the frosting was whipped and spread so professionally that it rippled and receded like ocean waves. The icing, she explained, was French vanilla and the cake was German chocolate. I am still not sure why cake flavors are named for various ethnic groups. But boy it tasted so good, kind of like I imagined she would. Too bad we ruined it though for Funkle.

We all sat behind Peter waiting for him to take a sip of his milk. He dug into the cake like his mouth was a construction crane scooping up big chunks of concrete, savoring each bite. Finally he grabbed the red pint of milk but then he simply put it down without drinking it. First, he nearly licked the plate clean, scooping up each crumb of cake but still no drink. We were dying with anticipation.

Mrs. Boone restored order.

"OK children, back to school time. Happy Birthday Mr. Funkle. Welcome to the seventh grade boys and girls! Is everyone happy to be starting a new school year?"

Groans

Kenny whipped a spit ball made from napkins at Peter who still hadn't imbibed his milk.

Mrs. Boone continued as if she saw nothing, "OK, why don't I go around the room and find out about everyone's summer vacation? Molly?"

Molly whispered, "Well me and my family...."

In my memory it's as if Molly's voice drifted off as Peter grabbed his milk container and finally drank from it. He drank the whole carton as if it were the last drink of water in the desert. The guys and me watched him as he leaned back and gulped it...glub, glub, glub. Even the sound was in slow motion.

Peter finished, licking his lips. The looks on our faces were like we had just been released for summer vacation and Christmas vacation and the hottest girl let us feel her up, all wrapped up into one moment. He had just drank the whole Ex-Lax-infused milk!

So now the wait began. Waldo stuck to Peter like glue that day. I hung back but I must admit it was like watching ketchup drip. When were the shits going to kick in?!

At lunch later, Peter sat alone eating his double-decker pastrami sandwich with potato chips like he did every day.

Peter...now there was a beautiful soul, at least in retrospect. Some impressions do change with time, unless of course it's Waldo and then, not so much. Once a dirty-ass snaggle-tooth, always a dirty-ass snaggle-tooth --

Peter Funkle had saucer-like blue eyes the color of topaz with double-rowed dark brown eye-lashes, just the longest you had ever seen. His hair was jet black and sort of shapeless as it draped over his right eye. It was really shiny and sometimes just plain greasy. He was very tall for his age -- I would venture like close to six feet. But he hunched over so much that no kid would ever really be intimidated by his size the way one really should have been. Low self-esteem will shrink any giant, any day. Funkle's chest and stomach were massive. I'm not sure how much was fat -- his belly definitely shook with each step -- and how much was frame. Regardless, he was fat. His skin was perfect, ivory white with just a hint of rose on each cheek. Honestly, if he was thinner, he may have been a lady-killer. Roulette, it's just a spin of the wheel, that and macaroni and cheese. The crazy thing about Pete or Funkle or Funkle Fattie, is that his voice was so soft. For a big kid, he just sounded so much like one of those cute orphans in that Christmas movie that your mother makes you watch every year...over and over and over again.

"May I please have some more porridge, sir," the little

orphan chimes on the screen, like a young tenor in the English choir.

I digress. Memories don't always follow chronological sequence.

Suddenly Kenny kicked my shin under the table.

"Hey man, why you kicking me, man," I balked.

Kenny with a wide-eyed grin pointed, "Look at Skunka!"

Suddenly Peter was holding his side. With a big thump, he toppled out from under the cafeteria table and ran half crooked to the bathroom. Kenny was hysterically laughing as Peter left the sounds of a big, wet fart trail all the way to the bathroom. The lunchroom of the entire seventh grade class was in stitches. It was a humiliation for the ages.

Incidentally, I should clarify if it isn't abundantly clear yet, we never called him Peter Funkle. Sometimes we called him Chunka-Chunka-Funkle but that was only on nice days. Mostly I would call him Funkle Fattie or Skunkle Funkle unless I wanted something...but that's later. Occasionally, I'd call him Peter.

Peter was so mortified that he ditched school after the Ex-Lax debacle and ran home. So of course, what did we do? Well being the reliable thugs that we were, we ditched school also and followed him. Actually we chased the poor kid. He tried so hard to run but he was hampered by the cramps in his side, not to mention a hundred extra pounds. Peter, crying by this point, suddenly lost control of his bodily functions. It was really disgusting, I must admit. He was walking crooked essentially trying to hold in his poop which was now dripping down his khaki (no pun intended) pants. The poor guy just couldn't win. What a way to usher in your twelfth birthday. But you know we just didn't care at the time, birthday or not, he was always fair game. This was the best thing since Mrs. Boone's peek-a-boo boobs. We were in our glory now. The good thing for Peter, at least we kept our distance now because we were so grossed out, a little consolation for the feces-covered guy.

Mentally challenged Waldo screamed, "Eeeiow, Skunkie-Funkie is crappin' in his drawers. Man, that's so screwed up."

Vocabulary wasn't his strong suit, maybe it was the crooked teeth that impaired his search for real words.

He continued, "Funkle-Fattie! Man you smell. CHUNKA-CHUNKA poop that's what you are! Peter-Poopie! Eeiow, haha!!!

We teased Waldo later for the new "poopie" nickname. That was never uttered again. Poopie! Even we thought that was uncool!

Peter stumbled until he found a tree. He hid behind it and cried. His pants were stained with brown now. Of course there was no real way to hide Peter. We just left him this time. If I could go back and change things, I would have told him two things: first, never hide and second, don't ever let them see you cry. It's like fuel for the fire. It just made us more pumped up and gave us more false power over him. But I can't go back.

I think the trail of shit running down his pants had kind of killed the fun for us anyway. We were over it. Lucky day it was indeed for Peter.

Chapter Three

Peter lived on the other side of town. My side was marred by a big eye-sore of rail-road tracks and trash heaps. Peter's, ironically was much more idyllic. Although an idyllic picture no matter how beautiful, doesn't always reveal the hell that inspired it.

The scenery for Peter Funkle was a kind of small town, could-be-anywhere '70s suburbia. The neighborhood consisted of somewhat cartoon-like cookie-cutter homes speckled with bright colors. Baseball caps bounced around on little boys who played in the area. A quick scan might reveal two cars in each driveway and a family heading to a picnic.

I may be taking poetic license with this part of my recollection, but for me, during my life at that time, it seemed that far apart. Peter lived with the picnic people and I lived with train-transients and trash.

Peter and his rough-around-the-edges mom sat at the breakfast table eating. It was the last day of school before summer break. The end of seventh grade was finally here. As Peter ate his cereal, he couldn't help but ponder in amazement how he had survived one more year of hell that began with Ex-Lax. He shoveled the Honeycombs into his mouth. He seemed sullen in the silence.

Pete's mom was running around doing so many things at once, a sip of coffee, a re-application of lipstick, juice for Peter.

She remembered to stop for Peter, "Peter, honey, are you

O.K.? Just one more day of those nasty guys -- Next year you'll be in a new school with older gifted children..."

He broke down suddenly into sobs.

"I hate them, I hate them!! I'm a lard-ass. Why can't I just be like all the other guys?"

Mrs. F. slammed her coffee cup down with authority, "Oh Peter no, don't cry! Big guys don't cry. You're a smart, absolutely gorgeous inside and out boy...soon to be a hot hunk-a-man...hunk-a-Funkle...so stop blubberin' like a little girl...please, for me?"

Peter laughed and wiped his tears. Mrs. Funkle kissed his forehead arrogantly because she thought she had it gotten right this morning.

Mrs. Katie Funkle...now there's a mom for the records. We all knew her as Mrs. F. She worked at the high-school which was part of the magnet gifted program which kids could enter into in eighth, where Pete incidentally, was headed...no passing go. Mrs. F. was tough and not one to be messed with. She kind of looked like a cross between Sabrina from "Charlie's Angels" and Cher. Sort of a smart girl and dominatrix all bound into one package. She was cool too. She rode a motorcycle to school. What mom did that in our neighborhood? And if you angered her -- as in messed with her son -- she would rip into you like the fence that slices your pant's seat when you're not supposed to be jumping it. Ouch! In later years I would fantasize about finding that kind of chick. But then again I fantasized about every possible type of chick.

Mrs. F....you could kind of sense when she was present in the room even if you couldn't see her. I surmised at the time, maybe she had to be tough since there was no Mr. F.

She continued, "I'm not gonna let any little punk-ass kids kick my son's ass 'cuz I'll just have to create a new set of balls for all of 'em!"

Pete blushed and returned with, "Mom! You're crazy!!!"

She continued, "Finish your breakfast. You're coming to work with me today. You can sit and read."

"Huh? The boring text books you always make me read! I'm twelve," Peter protested as milk spotted the sides of his strawberry-colored lips.

"That's right! Challenge that old noggin!"

Mrs. F.. waited for some response but there was none.

So she relented, "OK. You can come with me to collect the uniforms from the cheerleaders."

Peter laughed.

"Yeah... I thought that would get a smile...you stud you... Let's go," Katie was amused by her own job-well-done.

Mom and Peter grabbed their things and headed out the door. One could almost hear Cher warbling "Half Breed" in the background as they made the walk to the big beat–up motorcycle that sat in front of the house. Mrs. F. mounted the rusty hog first and with a little help, Peter boarded. They followed the routine: donned helmets, revved the engine and blasted off. Peter loved this part, partly because the speed was intoxicating, but also because he felt like an anonymous superhero under the helmet and for as long as it took to ride to school, he wasn't Funkle Fattie.

Mrs. F. always drove like she was on the open highway. And if you happen to be one of the neighbors who left a ball or a catcher's mitt too far out from the edge of your yard to where it hit the street, screw you. It was dust. It was all too common at the time to hear one of the neighbor's kids, whine to their mom:

"Mom, she ran over my autographed mitt!"

And then...

"Well, it'll teach ya next time to take your things in after you're finished playing!"

All the neighbors knew it.

Along the ride, when Peter relaxed into it, he would throw one arm up in the air to catch the wind, a momentary reprieve in an otherwise sad life.

Mrs. F. parked the bike at the Lincoln High School lot. She hugged his shoulder tightly as they walked into the school. She knew that no kid would mess with her son if she was there so she always made sure to stand right beside him.

He walked the halls keeping his head down, trying not to make eye contact with any of the kids for fear that they would tease him. As he walked, his striped polo shirt was riding higher and higher threatening to reveal a very cavernous belly-button.

Mrs. F. marched Pete into the secretary's office. Ruth the secretary sat at her desk smiling that all too glib, closed-mouthed smile that made me hate secretaries back then. Well at least that was one group I didn't have wet dreams about...well not until later when I discovered the hot-secretary-turned-dirty-student dream. But I digress in my telling of the tale.

Mrs. F. directed Peter toward the chair and approached Ruth.

Ruth DiBene...now there's someone I'd rather forget. Ruth the secretary, I don't know how memorable she was as I may have blocked her out because she was actually an integral part of that horrific time in my boyhood. Here is what I do remember. She had chocolate brown hair that was cut short and parted on the side. And she had a giant, brown mole on the end of her nose which only drew more attention to its length. Her skin was olive-toned. I think she was Greek or Italian. And she wore ugly patterned polyester dresses with bras that were too big so her boobs weren't supported. She was sweet enough I guess. I just didn't like her. I was very suspect of people at that time especially the adult kind who seemed to have some secret that they weren't willing to share with me. I think now, in retrospect, she was just happy and this wasn't a secret I understood yet.

Ruth burst out with glee in a thick Massachusetts accent, "Good Morning Katie. Well who is this? Hi Peter. How are you? My goodness you are getting to be such a big man. Well I bet pretty soon the girls won't be able to resist you, huh?"

Mortified, Peter answered, "I dunno."

Mrs. F. motioned to Ruth, "Ruth, do ya mind? Last day of school... he didn't wanna go...the kids...ya know? And I didn't wanna leave him alone. He's good, he'll read..."

"Of course, please, you don't even have to ask. Pete is one of the nicest, most well-behaved boys I know."

Then she turned to address Peter who was now wishing he was a superhero and could make himself disappear, "Are you going to be my helper today?"

"Yes Mrs. DiBene. Thank you. I'll be quiet," he obliged.

Ruth gestured to Katie as if to indicate how adorable Peter was like he couldn't see what they were doing. Mrs. F. patted her on the back and crossed to Peter as the school bell unevenly chimed.

She gave him the mom list, "Now hon' I have to make some final calls for colleges for a couple of kids, sign out the cheering uniforms, finish some disciplinary paper work and then I think you and I will blow this clambake early. Whaddya say...lunch at Fred Derby's ... Good?"

"Yeah, sounds groovy. Love ya, Mom...thanks."

Suddenly, Coach Wilson barged in.

Coach Wilson...what a character he was...still is today! Always tan whether it was summer or the dead of Winter in Ipswich and always donned in some varsity letter-man jacket --even today. He stood more than six feet tall, weighed in at a mere three hundred pounds and was never one who you might describe as a gentle giant. We never saw him smile, as handsome as he was, although he occasionally, charmingly, lifted his lip like Elvis. That's when he was amused by something. That guy was a real formidable presence. See I am reminded once again that this is another example of Roulette. Had Wilson been Funkle's dad, not only would no one have ever messed with him, but no matter how fat Pete was, his name would not have rhymed with skunkle and we probably would have picked some other poor sucker to torture. But as it turns out -- Roulette, just the luck of the wheel.

"Back at you, babe. I'll be back in a few hours."

She stopped almost flirtatiously at Coach's face. "Oh hi Coach."

And then she blew him off -- a turn-on every time for any guy. Especially when you are Katie Funkle flaunting your figure in skin tight jeans.

"Thanks, Ruth!"

Then she turned half-back, "Coach you need to keep your boys away from my cheer-squad!"

Coach gave his best Elvis lips as he spoke, "Hormones are ragin' Mrs. F. I only coach 'em how to play the game-"

And true to Mrs. F., half-Sabrina, half-Cher, she responded, "Yeah I bet you do."

And with that, she exited. Coach was flustered, then as always, it was back to football.

He turned to Peter, "Hey there, guy. You're getting pretty big, huh? Mom's feeding you good?"

More mortified at any further focus on him, Peter whispered, "Yeah."

"You gonna come try out for me?"

Peter couldn't handle anything but that day, "Huh? Nah."

But nobody could tell Wilson how it was going to be.

"We'll see!"

He patted Pete on the back but since his arms were so huge, he nearly knocked the boy over. Peter pondered for a second in amazement.

Chapter Four

Mrs. F. and Peter finally sat enjoying the end of the year celebratory sundaes at their booth at Fred Derby's. Pete laughed at Mom's irreverence and for a moment, lost in his ice-cream, he was a happy kid, innocent. And then we showed up, again. This time we were there to finish some unfinished business or at least that is how we rationalized our stupidity. As we came charging out of the men's room horsing around, we spotted Peter. We walked by his table -- couldn't have cared less that Mrs. F. was there -- and just as we passed, we stopped and let out loud fart sounds.

I began the rant this time, "You guys what is that funky smell? Does it smell like skunk?"

Kenny smiled -- like the hot guy does -- when he spoke, "No man, it's chunka-chunka Funkle! Look Lard-ass is sittin' right there. Man, we better ditch. The smell is Funky! Man, Funkle what do you eat?"

We laughed big guffaw-like laughs, another round of torture successfully carried out. Then all of sudden Mrs. F.'s nostrils looked like they were rapidly emitting fire. In fact, I would put money down today and risk all of my degrees to say, yes indeed, she was a fire-breathing dragon.

Holy shit, it was 'Run, now!' or risk being annihilated by a fire-breathing cross between Cher and Sabrina!

We ran! We weren't that stupid!

Then I looked back and noticed that Mrs. Funkle, who was now chasing us, was also wielding a knife. Granted it was a butter-knife, but I dare any of you to challenge a butter-knife, nostrils flaring, fire breathing mother who is angry.

We ran faster. Again, we could get smart real quick.

In between the fire coming out of her nose, expletives and run-on sentences, Mrs. F. spewed warnings in lightning speed, "I'll kill you, you punks, if you ever come near my son again! Do you hear me? I'll have fried balls for dinner you ugly punks. You pieces of shit. You dirty rotten maggots with dung for brains. I will call every one of your stupid parents! Do you hear me? And Greeney, your grandpa will hear about his white-trash, loser grandson's behavior if it's the last thing I do you little red-headed freak!"

Oh yeah, you didn't want to mess with Mrs. F. on school grounds but Lord help you if you messed with her son off school grounds.

We scattered in every which direction. Out of steam and breath and somewhat deflated, Mrs. F. walked back into the diner to her booth. Peter was crouched under the table as pathetic as that sounds. She crawled under with him. Then suddenly, Mrs. F. noticed that some patrons were gawking at her and her son under the table. It's not that unlikely that this may cause some what of a scene: a really fat kid and his mom under a table at the most popular diner in town.   But 'F' was having none of it. The townspeople still tell the story to this day.

"What's the matter? You never seen someone under a table before?! Mind your own God damn business."

An old lady was so startled that she clutched her bag and ran.

"Honey let's go, Pete. Let's go OK?"

Then as she started to cry, she let out years of pain right there under the table with the entire patronage of Fred Derby's as witness to this moment in Peter's life, much to his horror...again.

Mrs. F., her eyes welling up, obviously devastated, looked directly at Pete under that pathetic table and let her thoughts all come out, "I won't tell you to forget it. I won't cook your favorite meal. I know this stinks rotten like spoiled fish and I don't know how to make it any better. I just don't. I try and try and try and I don't know why you have to go through this. You are so amazing and I love you so much."

She sobbed hard which Mrs. Funkle rarely ever did.

She continued, "You just go 'head and feel shitty right now. I can't fix it and I won't pretend to. It just stinks. I'm so sorry."

Then just as suddenly, she whipped up from under the table and in one swift gesture grabbed a cherry from her ice-cream and without pause hurled it at a rude, staring patron.

Then just as easily, she returned to the scene under that pathetic table.

"This stinks and I don't know how to make it better except to-- Oh let's just go. I'm sorry Pete. Oh God, I'm so sorry, I've just made it worse," she sobbed now.

Peter retorted in his inimitable, big man whisper, "Mom, please don't! Why are you crying! Just stop it! God!"

Funkle Fattie crawled out from under the table getting stuck for a moment since he was so big and then stormed out. Some people clapped -- or so the legend goes-- and some people laughed. Mrs. F., very embarrassed by now, suddenly finding herself without a cause, slowly crawled out. As she glanced toward the door as if to gather strength, it is said, as the tale goes, that she "accidentally" knocked a paper boat of fries belonging to those who laughed, off their table and stormed out. I will again bet money that it was no accident and it was probably more than fries.

****

It was late. It had been a long day and a longer year. Mrs. F. had just tucked Peter in and as much as he hated this practice as he was just getting too old for it, he let her do it tonight. He needed her badly now and they both understood this. She watched him drift off to sleep peacefully and then dimmed the lights.

The next morning, Peter and Mom sat at the table, the sun from the window making Pete's hair look like an oil slick. He squinted. Mrs. F. hurried around like she had to be somewhere. Yesterday, while it seemed far away now, was the pink elephant in the room.

Mrs. F. tightened her robe which was threatening to fall open.

"Mom, I'm gonna go to Salter's Pond today while you're at the dentist, 'K?"

"Oh Pete, no hon' you have to come with me. I'm not going to let you go to the pond by yourself. I won't be long. Maybe we'll go to the pond after."

Pete balked, "Yeah Mom, I know but I don't want to sit at

the dentist for an hour and besides I'm not little anymore and all the guys go there by themselves."

"Yeah well you aren't all the guys..."

Then she realized that separating him right now was the last thing he probably needed. He wanted to be one of the guys and who was she to deny him this.

"Fine, yes, you may go to the pond. Yes, damn it, you can go!"

Mrs. F. cleared away his dish and left the room.

He hollered after her with a new-found resilience that even surprised him, "Thanks, Mom. Don't worry. I'm reading a really long book. None of those jerks hang out at Salter's Pond, only old folks. Can I have some bread to feed the ducks? Oh and I think I'm just gonna walk there and back."

The fact that he slipped in the walking part was not lost on her even though he had hoped that he had couched it nicely and sneakily so that she might not react. She pounced back into the room with her toothbrush hanging from her mouth which was decorated with green toothpaste.

Spitting the green toothpaste, she barked, "Oh NO!! I'll drop you off and pick you up. How's that, smart-ass? How about I am the Mom here and you're the boy."

She spit into the kitchen sink and rinsed with that faucet.

"Mom, honestly can we just look at this logically?" Peter philosophized.

"The pond is only about a five-minute walk from here, seriously. Life has a way of creeping up but in case you haven't noticed, I am huge, not a kid any more."

Mrs. F. ripped a few slices of bread from the loaf. She ripped them for the ducks but it might as well have been Kenny, Waldo's or my head.

Peter continued with his thesis all the while eating a piece of bread here and there. Mom walked out.

A little louder than a whisper this time, he urged, "And besides, I think walking is good for me...ya know...considering I'm fat and all."

She returned buttoning her blouse, wearing nylons and carrying her pants, putting them on as she talked. Peter was embarrassed.

Peter grimaced, "MOM!!! Put some clothes on, God!"

"Oh grow up!! I have stockings on. But listen to me, you are not FAT you are just..."

Professor Pete intoned suddenly with a new-found perspective, "Mom, I'm fat. It's OK, I'm not gonna lie anymore. I'm Funkle Fattie. It's not so bad I s'pose. Anyway I just want to walk there, O.K.?"

"OK, listen don't talk to strangers."

Grabbing a knife off of the table, with fervor, F. addressed her son again, "Here stick this in your back pocket for protection, ya know in case any pervert wants to mess with ya. Now I'm only going to be at the dentist for an hour so if you need to leave the pond before me, I'll just stick the extra key under the mat. 'K? Otherwise if you're not back when I get home, I'm gonna come get you at the pond. So your little behind better be somewhere where I can find it when I get back, understood?"

Then she handed him a baggie for the bread.

Peter, excited that he had won a battle, responded "10-4. If I'm not back, I'll just make sure I'm right by the Salter's Pond sign. But I should be back. Thanks Mom. Love ya."

"Yeah, the feeling's mutual, kid. I'll see you later, you little hunk-a-hunk-a-burning love."

After smothering him with kisses, she exited.

Chapter Five

Peter walked with a stick in his hand to the pond. He
walked slowly because of his weight but he smiled never-
the-less. Almost to the pond, reliably, he could hear the not
far-off taunting of my pubescent scowl. Squaring right in
front of him, on my bike, I taunted...

In the back-drop, as if Salter had no idea of the madness
that was Tom Greene, I could see the pond.

Salter's Pond...it was the sight of the best of times for me
and ultimately, the worst of times, to coin a Dickens phrase.
Salter's Pond was kind of the town center for locals.
Everyone enjoyed it. It was large and picturesque. The ducks
were everywhere. The stillness of the blue water against the
marsh could always be counted on as a much needed respite
from life. In the summer it was usually packed but it was
early enough in the season that today was fairly quiet.

I intruded, "Funkle Fattie, Fattie Funkle. Man you are so fat
the ground buckles when you walk!"

I started doing unpredictable wheelies as if the ground was
breaking. Peter walked, chin up, ignoring me.
And then he couldn't take it anymore.

"Yeah well it looks like a mess a' carrots crapped on your
head."

Peter raised his stick at me. I must say I was deterred for
like a split second. Who was this? But then the bravado
kicked back in.

So I came back with, again lacking any sort of poetic or

story-telling ability, "Oooh what are you going to do, roast the stick 'cuz I know you ate all the marshmallows!"

Then Pete actually aimed the stick at my forehead. I wonder what would have happened if he actually whacked me that day? But he didn't.

Peter yelled, "Just leave me alone!!"

I squirreled my bike around him as if I was thinking about leaving. Then I took off screaming back at him...

"Eeeiow you smell, man. I'm not hanging around. SKUNKLE-FUNKLE. FUNKY-SKUNKY."

And I made the loudest fart sound.

Peter just stood there and whispered to himself, "Stupid moron."

Soon, I would need Peter Funkle more than ever, very soon. But for now, he was my nemesis, my punching bag, and I liked it that way.

Peter continued on to the pond. He was kind of proud of that stick. If he had only known that on that day, his intestinal fortitude had everything to do with me leaving him alone and absolutely nothing to do with the stick. Maybe the events that ensued would never have happened. It's funny the lies we tell ourselves.

Peter read his book while occasionally looking up to observe with fascination, several in-tact families spending a family day at the pond. He marveled never having known his own dad. Then all of a sudden, Nate Goodman, a paraplegic war-vet and a local known only to the town's people as Crazy Nate, caught his eye. Pete dared to stare at him momentarily, but when the man glared back at him, Pete instantly darted his eyes in the other direction. Needing to get away from Crazy, he decided to hop up and explore the area around the pond with his stick as this was one of his favorite pastimes. He picked up some rocks, puttered around and fed his bread-supply to the ducks.

Suddenly, catching his eye, glistening in the sun as if it were a mirage -- or in Peter terms, a giant bowl of Mac 'N Cheese after a long day -- was an odd looking, straight neck, King 1920's vintage saxello, an early model saxophone with a 90 degree bell curve. Of course at the time, he just thought it was an old instrument abandoned on the rocks.

So there it was strewn across a leather case as if someone was playing it and had accidentally left it there. He picked it up and looked around almost expecting a family member to dash back to claim it. Nobody did. So he inspected it. It was unusual looking. It looked more like a gold clarinet than a typical saxophone. Of course he didn't know the value of this piece at all. He bent down, holding it up to the sun to get a good look. As he dusted it off, he thought maybe he would try to blow in it to see if he could play the sax. He'd always wanted to be a musician. As he brought it to his lips, Pete looked around to make sure there was no sighting of me, Waldo or Kenny. When he deemed the coast clear, he blew hard really fast. But he could barely make any sounds and the sound he did make was awful. He opened up the leather bag. The stitching was frayed slightly but the bag seemed expensive. He could even smell the leather still. He noticed there were initials engraved into the leather: FZF.

Peter thought to himself: "Huh, that's kind of weird. I mean if I was born Funkle Fattie which is what everyone insists on calling me -- my middle name is Zachariah...so hey maybe this is supposed to my instrument. Wish I could play it."

Of course Pete was rationalizing his actions so he could instantly be the rightful owner, or was he?

Pete was so lost in thought now that he had forgotten that he was in a public place. He caught himself mouthing his thoughts. Embarrassed, he resumed his investigation only to find extra mouth pieces and a certificate of authenticity which he promptly shoved back into the leather bag as if someone was watching and someone definitely was. Suddenly he noticed Crazy Nate staring at him, which made him very uneasy.

Nate ... now there is a very memorable character. I can honestly say, I will never forget that guy. All the kids called him Crazy Nate although I don't think he was crazy at all. You know how in some communities there is that one person that knows everything there is to know about everyone in town? In our town that was Nate. In some crazy way, I would say, that this knowledge gives the busy-body in town most of the power. I think in this case that was never more true.

Nate Goodman was an odd, fidgety fellow (although bound to a chair) who was a local transient. He had dirty, unkempt hair and a perennial grin that revealed one silver cap on his right eye tooth. He wore all kinds of military award pins on his beatnik, army green jacket.

Nate looked youngish -- maybe thirties or forties -- but his skin was so weathered from the elements that none of us were quite sure. A paraplegic confined to his American flag decorated wheelchair, he claimed that the paralysis came from his stint in Vietnam. Given that we were never certain of his age, we were no more certain of his service in Vietnam. The rumor was that he had lied about his tour of duty there and it was Korea although some local Vietnam vets vehemently denied that. Most said that he was indeed a Vietnam hero, a sore subject which was still very fresh at that time in the American vocabulary since we were "technically" still fighting.

Most of the money in his "hat" was a daily stipend from the local vets who loved him so much. I'd say he ate very well. Some locals who were fans of Nate insist that he only showed up at the pond in his chair in early '71 which in their limited reasoning must have meant he served at the beginning of the war. In any event, while Nate was somewhat of a trusted local, he remained a mystery to most and I am sure he loved it that way. His home was Salter's Pond which is where the infamous meeting of Pete and Nate took place and as you will soon discover where the legend of Funkle Fattie was born.

Pete looked down at his watch and realized he was very late so he bolted out of there, perfect timing considering he was being stalked by Nate. He shoved the sax and leather bag half into his backpack and began running as fast as an obese person can run but he wasn't doing too well.

When he finally made it to his front door, Peter frantically looked under the mat only to realize that there was no key. This wouldn't be good dealing with the wrath of his mother. He opened the unlocked door gingerly and then rushed in with all the drama he could muster fully expecting his mom to be mad.

Mrs. F. was on the couch waiting for him but she didn't look to hot under the collar in Pete's estimation.

Peter quickly explained, "I'm sorry I lost track of time!"

She leisurely responded, much to his shock, "I'll let it slide. You are only ten minutes late, but next time I'm going to take you down! Besides, I drove by the park and saw that you were still there so I figured I'd let you walk home since you are Fatsy Funkle."

Peter blasted her, "Funkle Fattie. Fatsy Funkle?!..Oh geez, Mom keep that up and they will start calling me that name which is even worse. Fatsy Funkle! God."

After a moment of panic, he collected himself, "Anyway. Thanks. How was the dentist?"

Mrs. F. pointed to his dirty sneakers indicating that he should take them off before he walked any further. He bent, albeit with much difficulty, and removed his tennis shoes.

Finally she responded, "Oh just swell, I mean doesn't everybody just feel like a million dollars after a visit to the dentist?"

Peter tackled the sofa, nearly toppling his Mom.

She gasped, "Peter, Jesus!"

Excited, he decided to break the news, "I found a saxophone on the rocks. It has a certificate of authenticity and everything from like the 1920's. What? Is that stupid?"

Feeling obliged to care, she answered, "No, that's good. Whaddya gonna do with it?"

"Play it," Pete answered resolutely.

He would learn to play it.

"Pete, it's probably got germs all over it and besides you don't know how to play."

Pete retorted, "It's not germy. I got some new mouthpieces. It looks kinda new, even though it's says it's super old, but I mean not germy, not germy, really. I could learn. Maybe you could pick me up a book on how to play it or something?"

He reached over to her and grabbed some candy-corn out of the bowl on the table next to her.

She mumbled, "Peter! 'Scuse yourself, my goodness! Well, alright, you can mow Joe Grady's lawn for the music book money. What do you think Mom's a bank?"

Caving to the sight of her son's beautiful blue eyes staring at her, she softened, "We'll see. Go wash up for lunch. I'll make some Fluff 'N Nutter sandwiches."

Finally he blinked and spoke, "Groovy."

Then he ran upstairs to wash up for dinner.

Mrs. F. was asleep on the couch. Suddenly the phone ringing shook her awake. She answered it sleepily, sort of looking for Peter as well. Then, what sounded like a cat in heat howling was coming from upstairs. It was coming from

Pete's room...horrific, feeble attempts to play the sax. Still rolling her eyes, she answered the phone.

"Hello," she said.

She recognized the voice, "Oh hi, Karen. How are you? Oh yes."

She was so distracted by Pete's sax-playing when she uttered, "Huh? Oh God no. I dozed off. Oh good. Sure. I'm sure Pete'd love that. Be a great fourth for us all...'K...great...no, no plans yet. Huh? Oh whoa...can you wait a minute?"

Mrs. F. was about to put Karen on hold and scream at Peter to keep it down but then she realized what Karen had just said.

She barked back into the phone, "Wait what? The Greene kid is goin'? You know what then, thanks for the invite, but that kid is bad, bad news, a thug. Look, yes I know all about his Grandpa. That's not a good excuse. Yeah, yeah, I know his story. Look...I know but...but...but Karen...oh God, OK fine. Fine, fine OK, enough! We'll be there, but I'm not going to be nice to that Tommy trash. 'K? Yes. I love you too...BYE!"

Mrs. F. hung up a bit annoyed by the bad sax playing and the thought of my presence at the 4th of July party. I was truly loved by all!

She screamed with all the frustration of the moment crammed into one word, "Peter!"

From upstairs, he hollered back, "WHAT?!"

"How 'bout a little peace and quiet?! Hey, I'll get you a

how-to-play-the darn sax-book, if you stop playing. NOW!"

  The cat in heat sound stops.

  "Thanks Mom! And, it's a saxello! It's a saxello, vintage."

  "Don't push it, Pete."

Chapter Six

Peter was watching TV on the couch. Mrs. F. entered holding something behind her back.

She whispered, "Shut your eyes."

He responded, "'K."

Then she handed him a book and of course a Hershey Bar.

He jumped up with a thud, "Far out! Thanks Mom."

He kissed her with a big wet kiss on the cheek.

"Right on. I love this stupid sax. I'm gonna get so good."

Peter ran upstairs with his book to practice and that's where the story takes a very interesting turn.

For the next several weeks, Peter barely left his room. Try as we might, we couldn't find him anywhere in the neighborhood which meant we couldn't get our rocks off torturing him. Waldo was never more grumpy. For me, it meant more time spent with my grandfather, Gramps, and that wasn't so bad. Peter, as the story goes, was practicing to be a Jazz legend.

****

Gramps...now there was a truly amazing man. I loved him with everything I could muster in my 4'11" body. He was a veteran of World War 2 and a decorated war hero. He treated me like I was the smartest guy on the planet. I try to carry on that legacy with my own son today.

Gramps and I would have talks about war planes and army strategies and he would ask my opinion about virtually everything, actually ask me what I thought. I also remember that he made the best steaks and he would carefully teach me how to keep the flavor and tenderness. I can still smell the marinade cooking.

My grandpa was a stickler about school and prayer. Although I don't think I really cared about any of that until I had some distance and life experience. He had been married to the greatest woman in the world, according to him anyway. Her name was Ellie Brewster and she was a real descendant of early settlers who came over on the Mayflower which makes me related to the pilgrims. She died of Cancer before I was born but he always talked about her.

Gramps was known as Skippy to the town locals, but his real name was Thomas Rattigan Greene. I don't think I have ever loved anyone more except for my son. My parents had left to join a cult in Guyana. I was utterly abandoned if not for Gramps. We never talked about them, my parents that is. I still don't really. I haven't ever come to terms with the abandonment however I am very thankful today that they didn't take me with them.

I don't remember seeing my parents past the age of four although I may have. But after they left, I am certain that I never saw them again. For many years I pictured them partying and drinking in some foreign country, taking on multiple lovers and doing hits of LSD as they worshipped their cult-leader and abdicated their parental rights. The thought of it angered me often because I thought it was unfair that they didn't have to pay attention to reality when I was forced to be all too enmeshed in it. I think eventually that rage became motivation to study and succeed and never be that which I associated with my free-loving, child-less parents.

It wasn't until my early twenties that I was told that my parents had actually died many years earlier in 1978 in Guyana in that same cult. They were part of a mass suicide only four years after that life-changing summer of 1974. Honestly, I'm glad I was lied to. I don't think I could've handled it at the time. Sometimes I do get angry though at the stupidity of my life and some of the cards I was dealt. But I never regret having my Gramps.

So each day during what seemed like most of that summer, Mrs. F. would go upstairs and try to lure Peter downstairs by making food bribes or promises of more independence on his walks. The result was always nothing. He was obsessed with that instrument. The best Mrs. F. could do, she concluded, was to support him and make sure she sprayed his fowl smelling room every so often. But each day she would go up there to check if he was breathing and each day she found him practicing.

Occasionally, when Mrs. F. wanted to listen, she would work around him picking up his socks that seemed to be scattered in a perfect circle around him or she would collect dishes of leftover Mac 'N Cheese and the occasional smattering of candy-corn. On a given Tuesday he could be found on his bed, supine, but playing. On a Wednesday he might be found standing at his window and on a Friday moving around like his room was a stage. But no matter what time or what day it was he could be found doing one thing: practicing that darn sax. It was like an appendage on his face. It always seemed to be hanging from his mouth, not unlike the Camels I learned to love.

Mrs. F., it turned out, was happy about one thing, the cat in heat sounds had stopped. This meant that she could again open his window in that hot summer New England heat, without scaring the neighbors. The Funkles didn't have air conditioning after all and the smell of one very sweaty Peter and many dirty socks was not a good combination. Mrs. F. chose to lay low about the hygiene issue because she had never seen him so passionate about anything. He seemed actually happy. This was a very new side of her son -- except if she was feeding him which always cheered him up. But this was Peter actually pleasing himself and aside from a little concern over the obsessive nature of it all, she thought that it must be a good thing. She chose to allow it with a careful, watchful eye.

We, the evil guys, couldn't care less however about some dumb instrument. Peter was ruining our summer. What were we were supposed to do if we couldn't chase or beat up Funkle Fattie? It was a very boring couple of weeks. When I did leave my grandpa to join Waldo and Kenny, they were mostly smoking Camels and making out with girls -- not in that order. So I, as previously mentioned, learned to smoke unfiltered Camels that summer. I didn't like smoking at first and I was beginning to realize I didn't like much about my friends or my life. However I was very unprepared for that feeling. So I just went on like everything was great. Coping was sort of out of the question when I was twelve.

After being finally satiated with the monotony of Waldo, Kenny, cigarettes and no Funkle Fattie, I finally figured out where he was hiding.

It was late in the morning on one exceptionally hot Summer day. Waldo and Kenny had gone to the beach with Kenny's dad so I was left to my own devices. Knowing now that Peter was stuck in his bedroom, I hopped on my bike and headed to his music cave. I couldn't take the Fattie withdrawal anymore.

Peter was propped up on his bed which was positioned parallel to his open window. He was again practicing that sax. He played while peacefully looking out at the view.

Suddenly he was interrupted by noise downstairs. And then he saw my image which he had managed to avoid for many days. Back to reality with one toss of the pebble, I stood at the foot of Funkle's house doing wheelies on my bike while angrily pelting his window. I wanted to needle him so badly.

I teased with fervor, "Yo Fattie Funkle. Is that you? Did I just see you playing a flute? HAH HAH!! Funky Skunky, you are even more fun than I'd planned. FUNKLE FATTIE, THE FLUTE PLAYER...Funkle Fattie the flute player, haaahhaaaaa!"

Pete heard and saw me but found more solace in just continuing to play. Suddenly all the guys showed up which was a surprise to even me.

"Hey man, thought you guys went to the beach," I quipped.

Waldo barked, "Yup and we're back. What's up with Fattie?

Is he too big to fit outside his door? Why is he stuck up in his room?"

Kenny motioned for them to shush, "Listen."

And suddenly we heard saxophone harmony dancing out of his window. None of us would admit it was any good, but it was.

Kenny broke the mood by hollering, "Hey fat boy. You big fat sissy. Now I know you must be a sis! You're fat, smelly and you play the flute. Why don't you come down here and play your flute Fattie Funkle, Flute Man or are you stuck in your room 'cuz you're so fat?"

Peter tossed his instrument on the bed momentarily to respond.

"Shut up! Just shut up! It's not a flute you Cretans!!!!

With that he slammed the window shut and we were shut down. It was so frustrating, this new Peter.

Waldo screamed with such rage, "We are going to get you Fattie Funkle Fart Boy. We're gonna kick your fat ass!"

Suddenly Mrs. F. stormed into the room.

She screamed, "What's going on in here?"

She leaned out of the window. Spotting me and my boys, she furiously responded. And we always knew Mrs. F. meant business.

"Get the hell out of here before I call your Grandpa, Tommy and tell him how rotten you are! GOOO! And you two, don't make me get my gun!"

We had never seen a gun but we weren't about to challenge her on that.

Peter looked at his mom incredulously and whispered, "GUN?"

I pealed off on my bike as fast I could. The other guys lingered.

"Awe your Mommy's gonna kill us! Funkle Fattie, momma fights your battles, sis boy."

Then they booked it out.

Mrs. F. comforted Pete, "You OK? They're gone."

"Yeah, but a gun, Mom, really?"

Mrs. F. left it alone.

She changed the subject, "You wanna watch an old movie with me?"

He muttered, "Naaw. Would it be OK if I just go to the pond for a little bit?"

She smiled, "Boy you really like that place huh? Well, yeah but you can only stay a little while 'cuz I worry. Make it an hour OK?"

Pete whispered, "Fine."

Peter packed up his saxello and walked out of the bedroom for the first time in a while. Mrs. F. waited by the window so she could watch him leave the house.

Chapter Seven

Peter contentedly fed the ducks. Occasionally he'd glance down fondly at his sax. Sometimes, begrudgingly, he would look up to acknowledge Crazy Nate who was again just staring at him. Politely he would smile back but never felt comfortable with the exchange. Finally Nate broke the ice.

"Hey sport, what's your name?"

Peter just shrugged.

"You don't know your name, Son, don't cha?"

Peter shrugged.

"Can you even talk, kid?"

Peter shrugged wishing this guy away in his head.

Then Nate continued this line of questioning, "Oh I get it. Is it the whole 'don't talk to strange people thing?' Yeah that's good, kid, smart."

Nate wheeled closer to Peter, frightening him a bit.

"Your Mamma probably told you that huh? Well me personally, I kinda like talking to strangers. Sides I ain't a stranger. All you kids call me Crazy Nate, so really that means I ain't unfamiliar, kid."

He got right up in Peter's face and intimated, "It's OK, you don't have to talk back. Unless of course you're scared o'me? You ain't scared of me are ya? I'm just like you, son. Only difference is I sit in a chair on account a'Nam."

Peter made kind of a frightened face.

Nate, sensing Pete's fear, broke it down for him,

"Military...Nam, the war?? Yeah, well anyway -- but I figure you and me probably got some crap in common right? You being on the heavier side, me in the chair -- I bet people give you crap just like me. Well I mean you don't have to nod or agree or nothing. I can tell just by looking at that big 'ol hump you do with your back, them sad eyes and that soft belly. Bet mos' folks don't even realize how big you are. Maybe if you just exercised that backbone God gave you. So do ya play that thing? I hope so 'cuz if you don't then you're just carrying it around and that's kinda weird, kid. I mean we all got our idiosyncrasies, but that'd be just weird. So assuming you do play that thing, will you play it? The sax, will you play it?"

Peter shook his head "No."

Nate didn't let up, "Oh c'mon kid that's not talkin' to strangers, that's just playing music and making someone feel good. Bringing a smile to their face, ya know. Unless of course like I said you can't play. Which, hey look I won't hold it against you. But do ya, do you play?"

Nate then played an air-sax. He put his whole heart into it until he got Pete's attention.

Peter nodded affirmatively, finally.

Nate happily replied, "Oh that's good 'cuz I was startin' to worry, kid. Hey that's an interesting looking saxophone I must say; I don't think I've seen one like that. Gotta be worth some change!

Nate then reached out to touch it. Peter protectively yanked it back.

Nate responded, "Oh whoah hey sorry there buddy. I was just gonna look. Well, can you give me a little sample?

Pretty please there, son"

Peter stared hard and then hesitantly raised the sax to his mouth. Suddenly he stopped and pulled it away.

Finally Peter whispered to Nate to explain, "I'm not good. I just learned.'

Nate reassured him, "Well you're a helluva lot better than me. I never learned nothin'. C'mon I'm sure you can play somethin'. Do you know 'Happy Birthday?'"

Peter inched toward Nate, a little more comfortable, "I just play stuff I made up. I dunno songs and random melodies."

"Oh hey that's impressive, son, a real composer."

Peter smiled at the thought. Crazy Nate may not be so bad after all.

"Well go head then. Play me that original, poetry-man."

Peter put it up to his lips and began to play a soft beautiful lullaby-like tune. Nate was moved beyond any of his expectations. Pete finished.

The myth goes that Crazy Nate let the tears fall from his cheek for the first time since he held a wounded comrade in his arms while the boy was dying in Vietnam.

Nate whispered softly, "Kid that was beautiful. I feel like I just got a massage. I'm tingly all over. Don't ever stop playing, kid. You got a real talent. Can you at least tell me your name now that we've bonded?"

Pete resounded at a barely audible, breathy level, "Funkle Fattie."

"Yeah! Yeah it works. You've already given yourself a stage name. Ya know like the greats, like Fats Domino or

Minnesota Fats. That's great, Funkle."

Peter smiled at this new perspective. He was suddenly pleased with himself.

Then he agreed, "Yeah. Yeah. It's my stage-name. And you're Cra-- I mean you're Nate."

"Nate Goodman. Thanks for the playing. See ya Funkle Fattie."

Pete answered, "OK, yes I should go. My mom will worry. Bye."

Funkle walked away, smiling at being called Funkle Fattie in a new way.

After watching Pete walk off into the distance, Nate lifted himself out of the chair. He leaned one arm onto the seat to prop himself up. And after years of "apparently" being chair-bound, he stood. He smiled as he watched his new friend Funkle walk away. It seemed that they both needed each other somehow.

Nobody but Nate was witness to the miracle of the sudden reversal of his paralysis. But as with most miracles, it got out. And in that single moment, on that late afternoon on a hot day in June 1974, the legend of Funkle Fattie was born. There was no taking it back now.

Peter began to run home. He ran until he ran out of breath. He was half way home when...

We showed up, again. Oh yes, we could always be counted on to ruin his day. This time we brought Bobby. So instead of three boys on Funkle it was four to his one.

Bobby...now this fool among us was actually a great guy.

Bobby was our new recruit from Boston. His parents had moved to our town late that Spring and Waldo had decided to make him our project. He was really rich and he had Shaun Cassidy-styled, white-blonde hair. The girls were wild about Bobby. He was very tall and built like a swimmer. I think he even modeled for a bit through high-school. He always wore tennis shorts in the summer with red striped, knee-high tube socks and white tennis shoes. His teeth, unlike Waldo's, were perfectly straight and pearl white, like an Osmond brother. He didn't talk much, but when he did, he could wrap it up for us in a sentence. It turned out Bobby was exceptionally smart. He just didn't want us to know that. On this now third move to another school, he was desperate to fit in. So we chose him, Roulette again. He was now part of the thugs. But it turns out that Bobby had a great family. After the summer ended, Bobby was never allowed near us again. Ironically, he and I met again in college and we're best friends to this day.

Waldo started, "Hey there Fattie sis boy. Did you play your flute today, sissy?"

Bobby tried his best to join in, "Yeah I mean you're kinda round, kid. It's vergin' on disgusting. Man, can you, can you... um, just go away. You're making me feel sick"

Peter just stood there staring at them. For some reason he aimed all of his venom at Bobby. He almost looked frozen, maybe even slightly crazy. We tried to get him to talk but he was so frightened that it began to scare us in a way. We couldn't tell if it was some kind of Bruce Lee karate superpower stance or he was just really about to crap in his pants. But either way, it was weird.

Kenny addressed me, "What's wrong with him, man?"

Then he spit in Pete's direction, "What is wrong with you, you fat Funkle freak?"

Waldo began to kick Peter in his back side. I wasn't sure how I felt about this sudden escalation of violence.

Kenny blurted out, "Talk you big fat loser."

Then we sort of strangely began chanting in unison.

"Fattie Funkle, Fattie Funkle, Fattie Funkle..."

Peter looked ill, really green. Now we ceased. We were stunned at the sight of green-faced Funkle. Suddenly, out of nowhere, he began throwing up. But it wasn't normal, everyday throw-up. It was coming from every direction. It was like a tsunami in its force. To this day, I have not seen vomit project out of the nose and mouth with that much velocity. I'm surprised he didn't choke with all those holes in his face saturated with puke. I can still smell it. It smelled like candy, only putrid candy. Then as if grossing us out wasn't enough, he really messed up. Peter Funkle threw up all over Waldo! It was war. In boy code: If crapping and farting add to a boy's fun at twelve, getting puked on is a boy's calling out. In other words: let's rumble!

We all scattered in different directions after recoiling with disgust.

Waldo stood there looking like a mad-man.

"Eeeiow, gross... yuck. God damn it. Man this is so fowl. I'm gonna kill you now. I'm going to rip your fat face TO

SHREDS," he insisted meanly.

Kenny, now cowering behind Bobby after sensing Waldo's rage, chimed in on the "fun."

"It's all over but the crying now, stupid!"

Waldo screamed hyena-like screams, "I'm gonna get you! You FAT FUCK! I'll kill you!!! You hear me. I'll shred you!"

At this point, we took off. Waldo's rage was even scaring us. I mean it's not like he needed back-up to fight Funkle. As mad as he was, I was surprised Funkle was still standing there. Then as suddenly as Waldo had lost his cool, weirdly enough, he just turned back around. He kind of just quit being angry and rode after us. A stay of execution was granted for Funkle Fattie at least for the moment.

At the time I thought, "Huh, maybe Waldo ain't that bad. Maybe he actually felt for the fat kid and decided to spare him more misery."

But now, knowing what I know, I realize that Waldo didn't have his thugs behind him that day to help him feel tougher. He was just a screaming coward without us. This makes me feel so much more guilty for my part in the events that eventually ensued.

Peter stood there, shaken. We had physically departed but the terror stayed with him. Neighbors said that he didn't come out of his house again for days. I'm not sure because I was house-bound as well helping my sick grandpa. But Bobby said that it was like Funkle had just vanished for more than a week.

I think we really scared him that day. No, I know we scared

him to half to death. He seemed more scared than he'd ever been. Maybe it's because he was slightly vulnerable after a good day with Nate. Maybe it's because he felt powerful and at the same time, defenseless when Nate put a new positive spin on his name. But it was like he felt like we were closing in on him, getting angrier. Looking back now, he was right-on, dead-on to be more precise.

Peter fell to the ground and put his head in his hands. After a brief moment he looked up at the sun, wiped his face, and with that signature resilience that he didn't even recognize in himself yet, dusted off and began walking home again. He was covered in orange-colored puke.

Chapter Eight

Peter entered his house. Mrs. F. lay on the couch watching TV. Enjoying her Mac 'n Cheese, she said nothing to Pete but merely engaged in her TV show. When she finally acknowledged her son with a smile and a nod, she put her index finger up to her mouth as if to say "sssh" and slid Pete an empty bowl that she had waiting for him. She pushed the serving platter over to him and scooped some macaroni into the bowl, while still watching TV. She was watching "The Mary Tyler Moore Show" after all. Nothing distracted Mrs. F. from "Mary."

Peter refused the food.

"No thanks."

Now Mrs. F. paid attention.

"What? "You gotta eat. Are you O.k.? Did those little shits give you trouble today 'cuz?"

"No, mom, just drop it."

Mrs. F. was in bad-ass mode now. She noticed his pants and exploded, "That's it! I've had it!!! Do you hear me? Was it that Tommy kid? Huh?"

Peter bristled, "I'm just not hungry!"

She squared her eyes right on his baby blues, "Alright but just so you know it is a cardinal sin to lie to your mother. Do you hear me? I know everything."

Peter let himself fall onto the couch. He sat next to his Mom. After he braced himself, he opened up to his only real friend in the world.

In his inimitable whisper he confided, "Mom, do you think

God planned for me to be a musician, maybe?"

She worried openly, "Maybe. And his plan could include high-school and girls and marriage and old age and tons of stuff that we might not know now."

Peter continued, "But God wouldn't make me play music ... right? He wouldn't, if it was gonna make me look like a blubber guy or sis or get me more made fun of, right?"

She bit back, clearly done with this game, "Peter, what's going on? Your talkin' nonsense now and I dunno where it's headed. You must a' seen those punks. The answer to your question is, I dunno. No idea, really. I'm not God, for sure, I'm not God. But I know, number one, you are not a blubber or a sis -- not that I would love you any less -- but now little Tommy Greene, Tommy is a little light on his toes, if you ask me?"

Peter held back his laughter, "MOM!"

Mrs. F. recovered with, "Fine. And number two, if you like playing this damn thing and you are good at it and it makes you happy, you go right on playin'."

She handed him his dinner and he put it down on the table. They talked now facing each other.

Mrs. F. got up and turned off the TV in the middle of "Mary," a first.

Peter seemingly more upbeat, suddenly busted out, "I think I'm going to use Funkle Fattie as my star name when I'm a famous musician. You know like the greats...like Fats Dominu and the rest."

She walked back to the couch, trying to hold back her

laughter.

She politely responded, "Domino, silly, not Dominu. A famous Funkle, Funkle Fattie, huh? Hey I like the sound of that. Just uh, don't share that with the guys, Pete. As lovely as it is, ya know, just keep it to--"

He smiled. Mrs. F. handed him his bowl of macaroni again and this time he ate it. Boy, did he eat it! After puking up his guts, the poor kid was famished. Mrs. F squealed to herself as she realized he was sitting on her couch in orange-puke-covered pants.

Over the next several weeks, Peter made almost daily visits to Salter's Pond and of course we were there almost daily to usher him home. It became like our forbidden dance. Pete seemed like he was kind of getting used to it. And we certainly didn't plan on letting up. It was only our reality in this small town. We chased Funkle Fattic and Peter endured the chase.

One day, not long after, Peter had finished playing a tune he had newly composed. Nate, uneasy in his chair was moved again emotionally, by Funkle's music. Nate started to wiggle his toes and fingers. Peter didn't notice at first but when he did, it was quite dramatic. His blue saucer eyes nearly doubled in size. He gulped hard. Now, for Peter's benefit, Nate decided to relate this sudden "healing" to the power of Funkle's music and the sounds of his weird sax.

For affect, he burst out, "Kid, play one more, please I know you gotta go but please!"

Then Nate kicked his "paralyzed" foot out slightly from his

chair. Peter was petrified as he witnessed this "miracle." What was happening to crippled Crazy Nate? Determined NOT to puke this time, he would stomach his fear no matter what it took. But it's not like he didn't think the Salisbury steak was on its way up a few times.

Peter rallied as long as he could and then he cried out, "Nate I really oughta get going, BYE!"

He was ready to run.

Nate pleaded, "Just one more Funkle. Please it really makes a guy feel better, please."

Reluctantly Peter picked up the sax. He played it beautifully. Midway through the song, Nate "apparently" began to gain feeling in his limbs. He started to get almost crazed. He was acting like the leprechaun on TV that Pete hated so much. Suddenly Nate was up doing an Irish jig. Peter was so obviously frightened. Nate had to stop.

He exclaimed, "Kid, that sax you got there, it has some kinda healin' agent. It's like medicine. DON'T EVER STOP, son. PLEASE, PLAY, PLAY!"

Peter had just about had it by this time. He freaked out, put the sax down like he no longer wanted it and took off like a marathoner. After a minute he realized he needed to go back to get his prized instrument. Dripping in sweat, he ran back, only to be confronted by Nate.

Nate worked him, "Funkle, why you acting like a scared kid? It's special. Please play a little more. Maybe God talks to you through music, brother! I dunno but a miracle is happening! Don't stop, soul brother. You sound like a jazz great even though you run like a scared li'l kid!"

Peter reluctantly picked it up and started again. Within minutes, Nate was again out of his chair doing a jig, deliriously. Peter grabbed his sax and ran all the way home without looking back this time.

After arriving home finally, he burst through the door as if he'd seen a ghost. He ran straight up to his room. About to lie down, he thought to check the window to make sure he hadn't been followed. When the coast was clear, he collapsed onto his bed nearly soaking his favorite Batman and Robin bed spread.

After what seemed like mere seconds, sounds emanated from outside Pete's window. Timidly, he picked himself up and peeked out of the second floor window. Nate was downstairs staring right up at him. Without aid, no chair nor crutches, Nate beckoned.

"Hey, kid, Fattie, pssst, Funkle Fattie? Hey can you hear me? Hey, thanks man. Don't be scared. You and your sax damned near created miracles for my legs, yes indeedy. Now don't be selfish with that gift. Anyway, I hope I see ya at the pond tomorrow. Bye Funkle. Luv ya son."

Nate walked away and then suddenly began to skip briskly. He laughed to himself at this game that he had created to encourage his new-found prodigy, one Mr. Funkle Fattie.

Peter punched his pillow repeatedly as hard as he could. He picked up the sax and started to play through his pain. He just didn't want to be different or more different. But it seemed he always was, no matter what he did to fit in. A healer! Funkle Fattie was not in the least bit, ready for this.

After a few minutes of playing and some much needed calming, he stopped abruptly when he heard his mother scream up to him.

Mrs. F. yelped from downstairs, "Pete...PETE!!!"

He threw his instrument down on the bed and ran to see what she needed, most grateful for any distraction. It was exactly what he needed.

The next day with the image of Nate's spontaneous healing far from his consciousness now, he awoke groggy, startled by a noise. Wiping the drool from his mouth, he lifted up at the waist and propped himself up onto his red Robin pillow case-covered giant pillow. He wanted to see out his window but instead saw a pebble heading for his window right in his line of vision.

"Oh no," he thought "are those jerks gonna start teasing me everywhere I am, even home?"

He wiped the crust from his eyes to see clearly. When he looked, it wasn't the bullies down below like he'd expected but instead he saw Nate with several disabled, transient types, and war vets covered with flags and pins everywhere on their personage.

Peter decided this was worth rising for. What were they doing down there?

He thought to himself, "My life is getting weirder and weirder."

Upon further inspection, he noticed that Nate was pantomiming to Peter as if to tell him to play for these people. Peter waved them away with a big obvious "go away" gesture as he feared the wrath of Mrs. F..

Finally -- and only because he thought it might make them settle down and leave sooner -- Peter reluctantly began to play his sax. He raised the window so they could see and hear him play. He noticed at this time several folks had canes, crutches and a few even had walkers. One younger woman was also in leg braces.

The original tune he played was a cross between Miles Davis music and James Taylor's "Sweet Baby James." It was poignant and nostalgic but at the same time it was raw, an odd mix of folk and emotional Jazz tones all rolled into one.

Lulled by his own playing, Peter almost relaxed. But then he saw Nate who had just knocked the crutches away from one wino who now stood straight without aid. Nate cheered. Nate pulled down the pant leg of another man who had appeared to be an amputee to reveal a spontaneous leg growth. Peter began to feel his dinner from the night before rumbling and threatening to come up. He kept playing to distract himself from his own fear...and nervous puke. Then the "amputee" suddenly dropped his begging cup and cheered.

He exclaimed, "You saved me, son. You did! I am clear as day, saved."

He pointed to his "new" leg.

They all started dancing and cheering. The girl in the metal braces kicked them off and hopped beginning an Irish step-dance. Nate cried at the sight of these miracles. Pete, now carried away by the excitement, decided that in that very moment, this had to be real. He was thrilled with himself at how he could help these poor people just by inspiring them through music.

"Maybe these folks were so sad that it made them sick and when he took the sadness away, they were healed," he thought to himself.

He saw it with his own eyes and that was good enough for Funkle Fattie.

Chapter Nine

Over the next few weeks, things got pretty weird. Now
Peter was the Fat Faith Healer instead of Funkle Fattie.
People were lining up at his window daily to be healed. For a
few days he managed somehow to keep it from his mother
and the neighborhood in general but eventually as with most
events this large it was bound to get out. And get out, it did.

Zealous, passionate belief, in the wrong hands can lead to
danger. I had experienced this first-hand when my parents
ran off to join the cult. But I guess we are presented with
lessons over and over again until we get them. I know that
now. Although I hadn't quite gotten this lesson yet, I would
soon learn it the hard way.

It was a Saturday, fairly cool outside, I remember it like it
was yesterday because my grandpa's health had taken a
turn for the worst. I took off on my bike. I was running from
something and it seemed no matter how fast I rode, I
couldn't escape. I had heard the home-care nurse speaking
to my Grandpa. Basically, she told him in very few words, to
get his affairs in order. The panic in me that swelled, I have
never quite felt with such intensity, again. I was very
unwilling to accept this grim reality. Who the hell did she
think she was anyway? So I rode until I felt as if my lungs
were being stabbed with sharp needles. And then I rode
some more.

Mrs. F. heard some odd-sounding conversations outside her
front door. She opened the door to reveal mostly "ailing" or
"wheelchair–bound" transients, some with wine jugs in hand.

She glanced up toward Peter's room as if to say, 'Peterrrr!' while he played the sax unknowingly for his enthusiastic, if not slightly odd crowd. It should be noted that Mrs. F. looked up toward Pete's room with an expression that only disapproving mothers, long since the beginning of time, have perfected. Scary is an understatement when it comes to Mrs. F.'s perfected, disapproving look. I know because I witnessed it all.

I had been hiding in the bushes outside the Funkle residence. Winded from my physical and emotional journey, somehow I ended up at Peter's house. Why I was so enmeshed in his goings-on, I still haven't figured it out. Never-the-less when the preacher says, can I get a witness -- in that verging-on-another-language deep Southern drawl, he is looking for the credibility that only eyes who have witnessed "the miracle healing" can give. In this case, Nate was the preacher and unfortunately, I was the witness. And my eyes were wide and innocent as I witnessed people being healed with every Jazz note. It seemed like maybe for the first time in my life, God had heard my prayers.

Mrs. Funkle slammed the door at the site of Nate and his circus of characters. She quickly reopened it as if to confirm that this weird event was truly happening in front of her door.

People were hollering, "He's a healer man! I can walk, son!"

Other people were celebrating by doing square dances. It was bad enough Mrs. Funkle had to face some of the more conservative nay-sayers in her neighborhood on a daily basis. Most of them thought she was a hussy because she was unmarried and rode a motorcycle.

But now she thought, "They will really put me away. I'll kill him, that son of mine!"

Fed up, she opened the door again and stormed right into the party. I took a deep breath for these folks, knowing the wrath that lay ahead. Man, she was good!

Mrs. F., the renegade, made her way through the whacky crowd.

She shouted, "'Scuse me...sorry 'scuse me."

Now directly in front of the crowd, square in front of Peter's window, she took a deep breath and let out all of her frustration.

She hollered like a lioness protecting her cubs, "PETER! What in God's name is going on? And make it good!"

As I peeked, I crunched myself as small as I could in the bush. Startled, he closed his blinds abruptly. But I remember I could see his blue saucer eyes peering out. People continued to dance and sing outside the home. Some were even trying to entice Mrs. F. to dabble in a Dosey- Doe but she wasn't having it. It was clearly a dosey-don't kind of moment.

All I could think about was getting home to tell my Grandpy that I had the answer. Miracles did exist. I would set out to get my own miracle. I rode off as fast as I could. Mrs. F. finally saw me and turned to holler but then realized she needed to pick her battles. I was gone anyway in about ten seconds flat. I couldn't ride fast enough.

Peter waited, bracing himself. Mrs. F. stormed up the stairs and into his room as if she was Dorothy swept up in the tornado. But this definitely wasn't Kansas.

Mrs. F. reached out to him again, "PETER ZACCARIAH FUNKLE! START TALKING...NOW!!!"
And then again she reiterated, "PETER?"

He whispered in a husky sound, "What? I don't know. I think it's the saxello but I'm not sure. Am I in huge trouble?"

She continued, "What do you mean? You don't know?!"

Now consumed by her own anger and lack of clarity, she was chasing Funkle around the room. He cleverly used his bed as a shield.

She layered it on thick as if he was totally unaware, "There is a varied and sordid group of sickys lined up outside my door! They claim to be healed...by YOU! Care to clarify?"

Again she barked, "Peter?"

Finally he relented, "Well...um...Nate-"

She cut him off, "NATE?! Who the hell is Nate?"

"Um...some groovy guy I met from the pond. He was crippled then I played for him and he...well then he wasn't. Um...so he said to play again and then he was walking, ACTUALLY WALKING, Mom! So then he explained that it was the sax and then he...well I'm not saying it's logical, but I watched it happen myself. He..I mean he really did..."

Peter was almost out of breath from the excitement.

Mrs. F., by this time, decided that she had just about enough, "Peter, a musical instrument can't make someone walk!"

He retorted, "But Mom he brought sick people to hear me play and they were healed too. I know it's silly but I saw it. And what if it can? What if I can? What if God digs the music and now I'm like Dillon except a real healer."

He stopped just in time when he sensed that his mother was about to kill him! And he knew it would be a swift, bloody ending!

Peter stood on the island that was otherwise known as his bed because there was no other options that worked as quite as well as this make-shift safety zone. Every time his mother attempted to get up there, he jumped on the mattress so hard with all of his extra hundred pounds and she bounced off every time.

Mrs. F. verged on lunacy now, "Peter, stop it. Get down now."

She swiped at the air.

He protested, "I didn't even mean to do anything funny or voodoo or anything, but they did get better, Mom! So I mean I kept playing even though it was kind of scary. I thought I might be in trouble, like I am apparently. I mean honestly, Mother, what would you have done, turned these ailing folks away who maybe felt better for hearing my music?"

Peter knew he had her now.

Mrs. F. smacked her lips at him. First of all, she hated being called Mother and second of all, she hated it even more when he had a point.

She relented, "OK, smarty pants, get down."

He distrusted the current move on the Chess board.

Peter answered defiantly, albeit respectfully, "No."

She insisted, "Peter, now."

She started once again to climb onto the bed.

Peter, now sensing he was out of tactical options, carefully picked up his sax and began to play before his mom could say or do anything else. When he finished, Mrs. F. was weeping. Internally, he felt a magical joy that his music had such an affect on people, but mostly, internally, he was thinking to himself, "Yes she ate right into my hand. Peter: 1, Mom, 0."

Mrs. F. softened, "Wow that was beautiful. God's plan, huh Pete? Wow. You definitely got a gift and you didn't get it from me. But really, it's a gift."

Peter smiled thinking, "Game over."

Mrs. F moved to check-mate, "Now...you're grounded!"

Pete made a face as if to say, "Game over. Peter:1. Mom: The Win."

Chapter Ten

Mrs. F. walked very purposefully toward Nate, who was sitting in his chair at his usual claimed territory at Salter's Pond. As she stomped toward him, she noticed him tapping his foot to the imaginary beat in his head. She was onto his game. And nobody messed with her son.

She addressed Nate, "Why are you fillin' my kid's head with malarkey about healing that you and I know is not true, Mr. Nate or whatever your name is?"

He grinned widely, "Goodman. Nate Goodman. The kid in trouble?"

She was not about to get drawn into conversation.

She summed it up, "Grounded. You bet! And he has you to thank for it."

Nate realigned his respect muscles after all she was the boy's mother. "Look, Mrs. Funkle, I didn't mean for it to get outta hand."

Again, she was not going to let him charm her, "SICKYS WERE PARADING OUTSIDE MY SON'S WINDOW! By the way, why are you even in a chair? Clearly, you aren't paralyzed!"

Nate tried to remind himself as he spoke, that he also had a mother at one time, "Yeah, well I got alotta injuries from Nam. Sure I can walk but why should I? Anyway, I was just tryin' to show your kid how he makes people feel when they're around his sax-playin'. It's like bein' healed, get it? But I had ta show him. C'mon he never woulda believed Crazy Nate in the chair. And so what -- He did heal me in a way. For the first time since the war I had at least a second o' feelin' less dead. Ma'am, no disrespect 'cuz I know you's just being a mother to your cub, but that's healin' if you ask me. But I know you didn't."

"Ugh," she thought. "I shouldn't have let him soften me. Damn it!"

She winced in reply, "Um. Look, he's a kid OK, impressionable. Just cut the healing garbage, wouldja? I mean thanks and I get it, the beautiful sentiment behind your insanity, but enough."

He grinned again, "Done. Mrs. Funkle."

Nate pulled out some cookies and gestured to her as if to offer her one.

Extremely befuddled by this exchange, she answered, deflated, "No thanks. Have a good day."

"Sure thing. Always, Mrs. Funkle. All day long. Right here, spreading peace and love," Nate expounded as he tapped his foot to an imaginary beat.

My world, my life at the Greene residence, was crumbling. There was no trace of peace and love in this home. Instead, peace and love had been replaced by talks of death and dying. I sat at Gramps' bedside, with the hope that only a young somebody can muster. I was broken like a sparrow who keeps trying to fly with a bent wing. It was tragic really. Present at Gramps' bedside was his nurse, whom I loathed by this point because I blamed her for being the bearer of such horrible news, and the chaplain. I didn't quite hate him, at least not yet. But I couldn't look at him. His white collar reminded me, with every loud tick of our grandfather clock, that events had turned terminally serious.

I pleaded with my Grandpa to please fight the Cancer. And when pleading didn't seem to work, I promised miracles.

I cried, "Gramps, please, wait...you have to hang on. I think I can heal you! There's this fat kid who heals with his magic playing. I saw it with my own eyes."

I could barely see through the wall of tears that were now gushing out of my eyes so rapidly. But even my lack of sight could not protect me from the incredulous look that I had witnessed the nurse -- whom in case I haven't said it enough, I hated -- give the chaplain. She attempted to pull me away with her oily palms as if she thought it was just all too much for me now. But hating her, only added to my motivation to prove this witch wrong.

I screamed in protest, "No! No, you don't understand. I'm going to heal you, Gramps. I swear I will do it and I've never lied to you, ever. Do you hear me? Do you hear me? Please, all you have to do is fight just a little longer."

She pulled harder now at my sweater.

I just snapped at her, "Get off me, fat bitch!"

And just before I felt the chaplain's hand slap me hard across the face for such disrespect, I was able to regurgitate all that I knew was true, "You're all I have Grampy! You're it! Don't leave me Gramps, please!"

And then I just fell over wailing, crying uncontrollably, partially due to the humiliation of getting my face slapped by a priest, but mostly due to the fact that I loved my grandfather so very much. It was so painful that I could literally feel my heart being ripped into red, muscular shreds by the evil Cancer which was threatening to invade the only world I had ever known that offered me real, unconditional love.

****

Mrs. F. and Peter finished watching TV. Mrs. F got up. Peter struggled to get up from the couch to follow his mom's lead.

She addressed her son, "I just have to make a quick run to the store. Do you wanna come with or stay here?"

He chirped, "Can I go to the pond. I want to talk to Nate."

She could hardly believe her ears, "No, I'm sorry. There has been too much weirdness. And I'm sick to death of hearing about this Nate character. Who the hell is this man anyway?"

She turned the TV back on and continued, "I don't even know Nate, and I'm sure he's a swell guy but all in one afternoon I find out that my son is a sax-playing faith healer and there are crippled people lined up at my door-step."

Mrs. F. now flummoxed stepped outside to retrieve a Boston Herald Newspaper from her front step.

And without missing a beat, she finished her sentiment, "And you compose your own music and I didn't even know you could really even play yet. Why is your mother the last to find out these things?"

She turned off the TV.

Leaning on the TV, she finished the lecture, "It's weird, son, very weird. And you'll pardon me if I haven't quite accepted the "New Zoo Revue" of Nate and his circus. I'll let you know when I am ready to don my long sun-dress and pass the peace pipe while you heal people."

Peter threw Mrs. F. his best attitudinal response, "God, mom. Is that a NO? That's a no, huh? Look, I haven't been walking, Mom. I need to walk if I'm ever going to stop being so darn fat."

Mrs. F. growled like Linda Blair in "The Exorcist" before she has that weird violent throwing-up incident, ala pea soup, "Peter! God Damn it! You can take a walk up and down the block, for God's sakes. You don't need to go be a faith healer to walk! No faith-healing music and no Nate, and no pond and absolutely no surprises! Nod vehemently if you are clear. Are we crystal?"

Peter sighed at this, "Nope. Got it! We are crystal."

She was worn out, "Now, I'll be back shortly, so make it a quick walk. I'll see you soon."

Mrs. F. stormed out. Pete waited to hear her motorcycle engine rev and roll away. He ran upstairs, retrieved his sax and satchel, ran back downstairs and headed out the door.

Midway through his walk, Peter looked at his watch and realized obediently, it was time to head home. He took out his sax and marveled at it while he continued his pleasant jaunt. Within viewing distance of his house, the joy was short-lived when he spotted us, otherwise known to Pete as the evil bastards, namely me, Waldo, Bobby and Kenny. We rode into his space like a trail of red ants surrounding him. Peter froze as he often could be counted on to do. Again, he was very frightened of us. Although, at this point one would think that knowing the ensuing events would somehow lessen the anxiety for him, but it made it worse.

I started the melee and boy was I happy to unload my rage on someone, "Hey FATTIE! I hear that you own some kind of magic flute. Can I see it, fattie-flute-boy?"

We took great pleasure, we, the four evil bastards, in coming up with new ways to ridicule Pete and his name.

Bobby joined in, still learning to be awful, "You better stay back, Greeney. He might up-chuck all over you. Remember when he hurled on Waldo? Man, that was super gross wasn't it? Waldo, you had to toss your cords 'cuz you couldn't get the Funkle smell out. He let chunks fly. Argh"

Now Kenny had to up the ante, "Yeah you fat sis. I hate you, you smelly skank."

Then we could always count on Waldo to break in his steel-toe boots. He kicked Peter hard in his shin. Peter bent over in pain and suddenly he could feel his lunch coming up. He started talking to himself to urge it down. We didn't jump on the opportunity to make fun of him for the self-chatter because we didn't want him to hurl. It was disgusting.

I decided it was time to get down to the business at hand, "Hey guys don't bother. We came for the voodoo flute right? So cough it up Fattie!! C'mon give us the freak'n flute, fat-ass!"

Peter exerted a false sense of courage, "No. Fight for it, Greeney. And it's a saxello, you moron! Can you say it, doofus? Sax-ELLO!!"

But his stomach took over. He gripped his side.

Then he spoke to himself, "No Peter. Don't do it! Don't. Don't." Then he turned that familiar shade of green. He lifted his head in slow motion and Bobby hollered, "Oh knoooooooww. Ditch guys! He's gonna bloooooow!"

And as usual we all scattered except for Waldo who obviously wasn't the brightest bulb.

Funkle projectile vomited all over Waldo's new cherry red corduroys. Oh, it was like the furies had been released from the depths of Hades.

Waldo was fuming now as he held his nose from the stench, "That's it you fat piece of shit. I hate you."

He just ripped into Peter starting with his ribs and working his way to Pete's nose. I was more than happy to pound just about anything so I joined in with Waldo. Just as complicit, but not quite as innately evil, Bobby cheered us on from the sidelines.

Then I realized that this would ruin my whole plan. And I didn't have time to waste.

I tried to be the voice of reason now, "Hey! Quit it you guys! C'mon. I gotta get the flute, c'mon."

All of a sudden like Superman out of the phone booth, Coach Wilson appeared, all eight feet of him. He lifted us three by our shirts.

Then offering us a dose of our own medicine, "Kenny I heard your brother made a play for my niece Annie. Is that true?"

Kenny didn't follow quite yet, "Awe for fuck's sake. I dunno. Let me go, Coach, for I have you arrested for battering a little guy."

Coach dropped us on our asses and grabbed Kenny by the nape of his neck, "What did you say, son?"

Then Kenny, rethought his wise-ass ways, and alternatively responded, "No. I said no it wasn't my brother who hit on Annie."

Coach finally let him down. I noticed Bobby trying to hold in his laughter.

Finally, all us guys took a hint and ran away.

Waldo yelled back, "We're gonna get you, you fat Funkle up-chucker! You better quiver in your stinky drawers!"

Coach Wilson helped Pete up. Peter looked up at him now with a look like he had indeed just met a superhero. Peter was so happy that there was finally someone who scared us instead. He smiled.

The coach comforted him, "Kid you really gotta learn some 'defend-you' skills."

Peter laughed, "No kidding."

Then the coach made sure it didn't get too girlie, "I better not hear that you are startin' trouble around here, hear me?!"

The coach grabbed Funkle by the collar.

Peter winced, "No sir. I wasn't. I swear."

He maintained his authoritative stance, "Well get on then. Go on!"

Peter replied politely, "Yes, Coach."

Just as the coach was walking away, Peter put up his fists to defend his face as if he was boxing. He felt empowered by the big guy. The coach happened to witness this. So he threw a pine cone to an unsuspecting Peter, who unbelievably, caught it perfectly, like a hail Mary pass. Or at least that is how Coach Wilson saw any perfect catch. He turned back to Pete and spoke to him.

He said, "Hey Peter, always protect the face. And, nice catch, son, nice catch."

Peter smiled, "Yes sir."

Then the coach, in a moment of brilliance, bent down to face Peter.

He looked at him square and said, "C'mon. Rush straight for me, kid. C'mon son. Don't hesitate now! Give it all you got!"

Peter wiped away tear-residue and decided that permission to tackle was good enough for him. He squared himself to the coach and with all the rage he could muster -- and a little help envisioning Kenny and Waldo-- he rushed the coach hard, while grunting.

The coach nearly fell over mainly because Pete was so heavy, but also because he was stunned at his discovery. He knew he had found a winner.

He boasted, "Huh? Whaddya know? Whaddya know?"

With that, he disappeared like the superhero he was. Peter just stood there staring at him as he walked away, mesmerized. He might as well have been John Wayne.

Unbeknownst to Peter, I was circling back on my bike. I had a mission. I hit the brakes hard and turned around to reverse direction. I followed Peter. As I got closer to him, he felt me on top of him and picked up speed.

I only had to complete my goal so I reassured him, "Hey Pete wait, man, I won't hurt ya, honest."

Peter squared his body to charge at me. I used my bike as a shield. He missed and ended up tumbling.

As he recovered, he blurted out, "Just go away and shut up, Tommy. I have fists. I'll use them."

Confused by this new, more courageous display, I responded gently, "Pete, buddy..."

He reacted to the insincerity, "I'm not your buddy you jerk!"

I hopped off the bike and ran toward him, cornering him from behind. Funkle was startled.

"Peter. I ain't gonna bug ya, OK," I said in my new-found gentleman manner.

He didn't buy it.

I had to keep trying.

"Look, I've been thinking some and I thought we should be pals."

He was very incredulous, "Huh? You, Kenny and Waldo just let loose on me!"

"Yeah he's stupid, Waldo. Anyway...ya know...best pals," I said not really having a good answer.

He blurted back, "Go away Tommy, carrot-top, go!"

I tried a new approach, "OK. OK. I just promised my Gramps I would change my ways and he's sick, real sick."

Peter was softening just a tad, "Sorry, Tommy, that's rough but--"

I hung on like a rabid dog, "So well, yeah so, could we be friends, maybe?"

Funkle wasn't the least bit convinced but he answered, "I s'pose."

But I figured an affirmative response would at least get me closer to that sax.

I mused, "Great. That is great, Peter, really great!"

I turned to retrieve my bike and suddenly turned back...

I thought to myself, "Here goes nothing."

I hollered, "Hey Pete?"

He questioned, "Yeah?"

I went in for the kill, "Do ya think maybe I could borrow that flute a' yours, now that we're buds and all?"

Pete shouted, "SAX! Um no. Well, dunno, maybe some time. I dunno. I gotta go."

I was a rapid Doberman, "Do ya think maybe tomorrow?"

Peter was overwhelmed, "Huh? Maybe, dunno, I s'pose. I gotta go, Tommy."

Peter picked up speed and was off. I watched him from my bike, disappointed, but happy that I had a chance of getting that "healing" instrument. There was hope.

Chapter Eleven

The Labor Day picnic was a big event in our town. The sign at SALTER'S POND was even given an addition albeit not that original: LABOR DAY PICNIC. But it was usually a fun time for all of us. There was a Ferris wheel and food stands and nearly everyone who could walk was there. Distracted by young prepubescent girls in short-shorts competing in the apple dunking contest, Mrs. F. manned a booth that sold hot dogs. The school secretary, Ruth, was joking with her about some local election scandal where the man running for City Council had been romping with one of their cheerleaders. I'm not exactly sure why this was so funny but Mrs. F. and Ruth DiBene were in stitches. Ironically their booth sign read: BUY A BIG WEINER TO SUPPORT THE LINCOLN HIGH CHEER SQUAD. Did they not see the obscenity in that?

As usual, I was on the opposite side of the social setting. My evil boys and I hung out at the far end of the fair lighting cherry bombs off at the side of the pond. We loved that it scared all of the deaf old ladies. I was also chain-smoking unfiltered Camels as well. I had become quite good at it.

By this time Kenny was living in Carrie Spagnolo's pants on a semi-regular basis. She was the town tramp as far as the 13 year old set went. I think she was secretly taking care of Bobby as well, but none of us dare brought it up. Although Kenny was normally an arrogant ass, she puffed him up with ten times more bravado. With this even bigger ego, it seemed he was always starting with one of us.

Kenny turned to address me while Carrie hung onto him as

if she had no bones. She slowly worked her way down his body.

Kenny carried on, "Hey Red, one of the guys said you was talking to Fattie..."

I answered him with one eye closed, "Yeah, so?"

Then he asked the next most sensible question, when you're a moron, that is, "You a sis, Red?"

I burst out, "Shut up, Kenny."

Then as if she had a brain-cell to back up her interjection, Carrie chimed in, "Oh you guys, stop being so childish."

Kenny kissed Carrie. I was disgusted. I threw some rocks into the pond to stop myself from throwing them at him. It worked. He and Bobby started doing wheelies on their bikes. Waldo pulled out some cold beers and offered us each one. We all flinched and looked around because this was really defiant.

I asked him, "Where'd you get those?!"

He muttered, "The old man."

Having no back-bone, I took one. Kenny took one. The others followed. We lit up smokes, coughed and chugged some beers directly in front of the nosy adults who were at the pond. No one did anything so we thought we were the ultimate in cool.

Kenny continued, "So what's up with you and fat boy?"

"Jesus, Kenny, what are you jealous?"

Kenny lunged for me without missing a beat. We scuffled, still holding our cigarettes although we had the good sense to hand off our beers. Suddenly Father Michael, a local priest, walked up. Carrie saw him first. And with a cat-cough as a warning, she buttoned her shirt and wiped off her lipstick while we, completely unaware, kept fighting.

Then she coughed louder to warn us.

He jerked us by our sleeves, "Boys stop that! Put those cigarettes out! Where are your parents?"

We dropped our smokes. All the evil boys scattered on their bikes. Carrie stood there by herself. I managed to grab the pack of camels.

We were still breathing heavily from the skirmish.

Father Michael lectured, "Miss Spagnolo, where are your parents?"

Carrie, lost for words, answered sarcastically, "Church, Father?"

Somewhere on the other side of the fair, the crowd assembled by a tree, swayed in unison. Couples lovingly watched. The music trailed through the trees on this, the other side of the pond. There were no evil bastards here, only peaceful music-lovers. Nate weaved his chair around a very large man, over to a pretty girl with her mom and on to a sexy hippie girl. To each he extended his hat for the violinist who was playing the "Love Story" theme on stage. People were definitely in a giving mood. Although I am not sure how giving they would have been if they knew that he always skimmed half from the hat.

Funkle, leaned on a tree watching. His hair hung a little longer now, in more of a hippie style by the end of summer. He definitely played it up too -- the hair hanging in his face -

- it made him feel like a Beatle.

No sooner did the violinist jump down after bowing for the crowd, did Nate switch the signs on stage and empty the hat. Funkle donned the stage with his infamous saxello in hand.

The sign that hung between the two trees was switched to read:

Funkle Fattie's Healing Hymns

Funkle began to play. As soon as he got into it, you could hear a pin drop for a great distance as people watched and listened, clearly stunned at this kid's talent.

It seemed I could never get enough of him. I had heard from someone passing by that Funkle was playing so I had ditched the guys and rode over. I didn't get too close but watched only from a distance, kind of nestled behind a big tree. There was no doubt even to my untrained ear that Funkle had some kind of gift for making music. The only question I wondered was: did it really heal the sick?

Funkle finished his first set and not a single person was left out of the hooting, hollering and bravos...well except for me of course. Nate did not miss the opportunity to cash in. He jumped out of his chair and proselytized the word of Funkle.

Nate bellowed as if he was suddenly Reverend King, "Hallelujah, Funkle Fattie! Now that, my son, is medicine for the soul! C'mon people, every little bit helps. The fine lad continues to heal folks like myself and ailing folks throughout the world through his music. Dig into your pockets. Dig deep now! There you go Big Daddy. Awe, thank ya pretty little girl."

People, who at first were giving change, instead started throwing in dollars. And with that, Nate cleaned up. Ones, tens -- It was a full hat after Funkle's set. And the best was, Funkle still had another set to go.

Hiding behind the big tree trunk, I felt myself get weepy. I wasn't sure what was happening and I sure didn't want anyone to see it, but I knew something had changed in me after hearing his composition. It was like he composed these Jazz tunes that talked directly to your soul. You could hear them certainly, but most of all they cut right through the core of your struggle, whatever that was for you personally. And then for a split second I allowed myself to ponder that.

I thought silently, "That's it. That's his gift. Funkle had experienced such struggle that it allowed him to translate it somehow in such a way that we were all affected."

Then I quickly dismissed that very deep thought as it just didn't fit in with my role as an evil boy or my coping strategy at the time. But as with all repressed thoughts that do matter, it didn't go far. It wouldn't let me forget. I would have to address it someday. I would never forget that I was the cause of his struggle on so many levels.

Although I was feeling moved by my introduction to Jazz music, the feeling very quickly became secondary to the fact that Nate was jumping around -- out of his chair. He was really and truly healed from his paralysis. And while I wasn't sure if his claim that Fattie's music had indeed healed him, I wasn't about to wait much longer to find out. My grandfather didn't have time for me to second-guess my decision.

A woman yelled out a request now, "Play, 'Peace in the Valley!'"

Peter laughed and responded politely, "Um, well I mostly play my own stuff. Awe, heck I suppose I can play that for you. I think I know it."

People clapped. He leaned into his odd shaped sax. She smiled as he started playing and then she cried. She cried and cried.

While Funkle played, he had no idea that a young girl Sally Anne Gregor was smitten already. She had watched from the crowd, her big metal-encased mouth of braces, smiling and hiding nothing. She was the kind of girl that had you asked me then, I would've said, '…eiow, Sally-Anne is ugly.' However most adults in their wisdom would probably have recognized that with her long blonde hair and big blue eyes, she would probably grow out of that awkward phase one day and be very pretty in high-school. But at that time, she was super awkward and clearly could care less what the popular guys thought of her.

Tall and lanky, Sally-Anne was dressed in long, sky blue-patchwork, polyester bell-bottoms. She wore a crocheted white vest that hung to her hips and was adorned with long hand-made beaded necklaces. Her arms hung like odd, extremely long appendages out of her white tank top. Her honey-blonde hair was messily tied in mismatched ponytails. And nobody would ever know she had gorgeous blue eyes under her coke-bottle, black-rimmed eye-glasses. She carried a guitar in its case. The case had all kinds of peace stickers on it. Watching from behind the tree, I was actually a little fixated on her. Not only because she was so obviously enamored by Fattie, but also because she was new in town. She had to be. I mean everyone knew everyone in our town and I had never seen her before.

Finally after a long set, Sally caught Funkle's eye (the one that was visible through his bangs). She smiled bigger, if that was even possible. He nearly dropped the sax, but kept his cool and resumed playing. Casually, he looked around for the focus of Sally-Anne's apparent attention. When he realized that she was beaming at him, he smiled back. As soon as he hit that last note, he jumped down off of the make-shift stage. I decided that it was now or never. I made a bee-line for the stage but Sally-Anne accidentally knocked my head clear off my neck with her guitar-case when she turned to introduce herself to Peter.

I wailed loudly, "Ouch! Crap! Stupid girl!"

Sally-Anne and Funkle walked toward each other, an effort which seemed to take a nauseatingly long time. Nate jumped onto the stage to rile the crowd.

Ever the salesman, he proclaimed, "OK folks, he's only taking a short break. Go get your cotton candy and come right back and when ya do, sit your behinds down for some more lovely, healin'-type music."

The crowd, for the most part, dispersed.

Sally-Anne and Peter stared at each other for a moment awkwardly. It's like that thing you do when you're twelve and you suddenly realize, hey wait a minute, now I know what everyone else has been so excited about...the opposite sex! And when it hits, it hits you like a ton a bricks. So Funkle was a little caught under the rubble, temporarily. It took him a moment to catch his breath as he gazed at Sally-Anne.

I tried with all of my diminutive might to interrupt this fiasco so I could get my flute or sax or whatever he called it. But just when I was going in for the kill, I was stopped by the giant, dirty hand of Nate gripping my shoulder guiding me in the opposite direction. I had to ask myself, was he everywhere for Pete's sake? Not Funkle Pete just in general for Pete's sake. I was frustrated as all hell!

Nate bellowed in a paternal tone, "Hey son. Can I help ya out with somethin'?"

I was steamed, "Hah? Yeah you get your dirty hand offa me!"

Nate laughed at me, "Wow, you're a smart aleck! Don't you know that a man never cuts in on another man's action?"

I had to remain tough, "Funkle don't get no action, dummy. He's a sis! Don't you know that you're a crazy nut? Hey, how come you're walking anyway, huh? Was you really healed by that stupid music? Huh?"

Nate smiled as he spoke. I wondered what made him so happy. He had nothing to call his own, not even soap.

He looked at me, bent down real low and whispered, "Who's askin' huh? You ain't so tough. Tommy is it? You don't think that music is stupid no more than I do or you wouldn't be here. Yeah, I was healed in a way, case your askin'. What's it to ya?"

Suddenly he was walking me far away from Peter. I was kind of frightened of him but it added to my frustration as well. I needed that instrument and I was going to get it somehow!

I kicked a can so hard in Nate's direction. It whipped off his shins. He still smiled, the fool. In fact he was laughing as if Richard Pryor was doing a private comedy show just for him. God, he irritated me in that second! I lit a Camel, coughed up a lung and trudged off. I grabbed my bike and rode away.

Chapter Twelve

Sally-Anne was no slouch. She liked Peter and even if he had lost his ability to articulate it, she was determined to talk to her musical crush.

She flashed her metal-mouth grin, batted her eye-lashes that incidentally hit the coke bottle lenses of her glasses, and spoke, "Hi."

She kind of sounded like Goldie Hawn on "Laugh In." She sounded really dumb and giddy like Goldie's dumb blonde thing on the show, but she wasn't, she wasn't dumb at all. She was super smart. I don't know. I think everything just bothered me about Sally-Anne. I felt abandoned in a way. I mean, I panicked to myself, were we still going to call him sis and blubber? And quite honestly, girl or not, she was way bigger than me. I just wasn't happy about this new arrival called Sally-Anne. Of course my world was changing way too rapidly anyway and none of it was making me happy. And no one seemed to notice. I was just lost. My only hope was getting that sax.

Funkle found his voice again, "Hi."

OK, so they were finally getting around to uttering sounds. Far from profound conversation, but at least it was human-like for Pete's sake. It wasn't deep conversation, but even the Cro-Magnon man had to start somewhere.

While they conversed, I found myself raving mad at Nate. I had a conversation with myself as if it were to him. I bantered all the way back to the other side of the fair and then I just got really steamed. I skidded in the sand as I turned back around to go confront that crazy man.

"Who the hell was he anyway?" I thought.

Finally I reached Nate again and I was even madder by the time I got back. Although the sight of him and the reality of the confrontation scared the be-Jesus out of me, I was determined to give him a piece of my mind.

I looked up at his maniacal expression and blurted out, "You crazy man!"

Then I think I peed in my pants a little. The fool laughed again. What did it take to rattle this ass-hole? And then he did something odd. He gripped my shoulder and sort of hugged me and hung on. I was very freaked out. It was Crazy Nate after all. But at the same time, I think somewhere in my lonely little body, I felt that he genuinely may have cared. I didn't shrug him off. I simply stiffened a little bit. He just kind of hugged the back of my shoulder like a buddy. We stood there as if we were father and son at a picnic. It was weird. I looked around to see if any of the guys were in sight and when I realized that they were nowhere in the vicinity, I just let him hold me up. Honestly, I was falling apart. It was the exact thing I needed at that moment, although I never would have admitted it to him.

Nate then spoke to me out of the side of his mouth as if it were a secret, "You ain't that tough kid. You just ain't that tough. A hug's all ya needed."

Then he mussed up my hair as if to say, "Good boy."

****

Funkle had now graduated to full sentences with Sally-Anne.

He blurted out, "Um. Yeah. So, what's your name?"

She smiled, showing the little elastic bands that connected her lower braces to the upper ones. She spat as she answered, "Sally-Anne. Gregor, my last name is Gregor, that is. You play really good."

Funkle, not quite skilled yet with the women, answered, "Well. Um, so you know, the word is play *well*, not play good."

Sally-Anne frowned for a second in response. Then she pushed her glasses back up the bridge of her nose and resumed smiling.

Funkle kept on, "Do you play?"

She giggled, "The saxophone?"

He continued, now getting accustomed to full sentences...well almost. "No, um--"

He pointed to her guitar case.

Sally guffawed at her momentary lapse of memory that happens when you're hormonal. "Oh, yeah I'm learning some Joan Baez. I'm not half as good as you though."

They started walking. Funkle passed his mom's stand and without missing a beat grabbed three foil-wrapped hot-dogs, two for him and one for her. He was becoming a real man now!

Mrs. F. could not contain her shock at seeing him with a girl. I mean he barely even spoke on a daily basis! Ruth was tickled. I hated that woman!

Sally-Anne grabbed her hot-dog. She gushed.

"Awe thanks Peter! You're, um, super sweet."

Funkle nodded. He was too busy eating to come up for air. Rome wasn't built in a day. He just met her! Food was still his best friend.

She spoke for the both of them, "So, maybe we could have a band or something."

Funkle inhaled the last bit of his second dog and smiled.

After he burped to himself, he spoke, "I've never seen you around here."

Sally-Anne responded, very relieved that he had stopped eating so he could speak to her. "We moved here from San Francisco last week."

Funkle answered, "Wow that's so far away."

Sad for a moment at the thought of her former home she muttered, "Yeah. You don't know the half of it. It was such a cool scene. There was always a protest or music-fest or something. It was real groovy. And I walked mostly everywhere. My folks didn't have to drive me much. We lived right in Haight. This town is kind of really different for me. It's very 'Brady Bunch.'"

Although most of what she said was lost on him and he was still trying to figure out why someone would live in a town called, "hate," he thought he'd just talk about what he did know.

"Yeah 'The Brady Bunch' is super cool though. You look kind of like Jan in a really swell way...sort of."

She nodded and giggled.

He continued, "What grade are you in? I mean you seem like kind of older...or ya know sort of more high-school."

She giggled yet again, "Ninth, and you?"

Funkle thought he could handle a ninth-grader, so with a wave of confidence he lifted his chin as he spoke. "Comin' up on eighth, but I might skip -- skip ahead into ninth. Good grades and I'm way ahead in math. Feels like I'm in kindergarten sometimes. It's a cinch."

Sally-Anne desperately trying to keep this romantic as girls will do, made a suggestion. "Oh. Wanna go on the Ferris wheel?"

Funkle answered comfortably, "Well, yeah but I gotta play more after that. I think Nate arranged one more set."

Then she reached in and did it...

Suddenly Sally-Anne was holding Funkle's hand. He didn't let go even though his palm was sweatier than a pig in heat.

Then she bolstered his ego a little as she spat out, "Oh yes I know, my dad is a musician. I understand. I won't keep you from your art. By the way, who is that Nate guy anyway?"

And with that complicated question looming in the air, they walked off to the lighted wheel looking as all-American as the Weiner dogs Funkle was now attempting to digest. But as with all fairy tales, there was evil lurking.

Chapter Thirteen

The sun had set by now on this Labor Day that had been so great for so many towns-folk. People sat mostly in groups or with family. With sunburned backs and noses, they seemed to be experiencing that lull that you feel after a sun-filled day of Frisbee and too much orange soda. The kind of lull that you try to snap out of because it's still so warm out and the smell of dogs and burgers still looms in the air. Music plays and children laugh awaiting the local fireworks display. As I observed the setting, that's what it looked it like to me.

My mouth was dry from too many Camels and beers in the summer heat, I wasn't tossed though, I only drank maybe one and half but it was enough. I thought to myself, I will have that experience some day. Some day I will be a part of a family that gets to do that-- Family day.

But for now, I was an outsider, a punk. And I had to live it down.

On the other side of the fair, Sally-Anne sat now on her guitar case. There were very few people watching Funkle anymore but Nate was still there. The donation hat was stuffed and overflowed with green bills.

On stage, Peter looked at his new crush in the small crowd as he started a new song. He stared lovingly at Sally who was tearing at her cotton candy as she listened and swayed.

He shouted, "This one is for a...girl. I mean I'm dedicatin' it to her -- For you Sally-Anne."

Sally laughed and blushed.

He played the crowd into a trance which was suddenly and violently shattered. Sally-Anne and others looked over to view the loud disturbance. And of course it was my evil boys. I chose to back out so I wasn't there but I had to live up to my image. So I had been the one who tipped off the guys. Kenny mooned the stage. Waldo peed on the money hat. Bobby made baby-crying sounds.

Nate looked on, concerned. Some of the crowd started shouting, but mostly, families just moved elsewhere.

Bobby, getting better at being a jerk now, sputtered, "Whaaah - Whaaaah. Boo-hoo! My name is Fattie and I'm such a cry-baby sis!"

Kenny took it home, "Funkle Fartie!"

Then he made classic fart noises.

And he continued, "Play that flute, Fartie. Maybe it will heal your bad Funkle gas! P.U.!"

Funkle, I heard later, was mortified. Apparently, he tried to play through the humiliation but it was just too intense in front of Sally. Nate held back from helping because he didn't want to embarrass Funkle any more.

Waldo yelled, "Yeah that flute didn't help ya when you pooped in your pants all the way home! Eeiow it was drippin' everywhere."

Kenny added, "Yeah it was running down his leg, hah, hah."

Funkle looked at Sally-Anne who was now covering her face in disgust. Nate finally got up to stop the melee but before he could, Funkle bolted off the stage, sax in hand. He ran through the small crowd passing all the evil boys who continued to laugh at him. Bobby's laugh was particularly haunting and bellowing. You could hear it for miles. The way Waldo described it later, Funkle turned a deep shade of red and looked as if he was about to burst into tears at any moment. It's weird because I remember being retold the story and having a strange awakening occur. Since I was only hearing what had happened and hadn't participated, it gave me some distance from the situation and it actually, for the first time, ate at my conscience a bit. Were we that awful? But again, I had to maintain my persona even though inside, I felt kind of bad for the big lug.

Nate slowly made his way over to the evil boys. Bobby was about to hyperventilate from laughing so hard. Suddenly, Nate grabbed him by the scruff of his neck.

He exclaimed with all his craziness, "BOOH!"

Bobby jumped a mile. And about as fast as you can say, "Crazy Nate," they all took off.

Sally laughed at Nate and the boys' display of cowardice.

Coach Wilson strolled up to Mrs. F.'s barbecue stand.

He flirted with Mrs. F. as he spoke, "Hey Kate. Your son Pete's my next star tackle! I got my eyes on that boy. What do you think?"

For the longest time, there was a rumor that Mrs. F. was having relations with the eternal bachelor, Coach Wilson. We never really found out the truth though. He eventually married some stripper from Boston. She looked like a Playboy Bunny, like Barbie Benton.

Mrs. F. answered coyly, "Well. We'll see."

The coach laughed and walked away but not before he absconded with a very old Weiner dog.

Suddenly Funkle, stormed up to the stand in a rage and completely destroyed it. He threw the foil-wrapped dogs everywhere.

Mrs. F. fumed furiously, "Peter!"

Funkle expounded in an unusual display of rage, "I'm going home. I hate this stupid town and this stupid fair. I hate you for making me live here. Do you hear me! I HATE you!"

Then he ripped the BBQ sign into tatters. The only in-tact part read: Q

Mrs. F. was having none of this behavior. She scolded him, "Peter, stop this right now. Ruth, I am so sorry."

She then grabbed Peter by the arm as if he was a soldier and she was his sergeant. She yanked him to the side.

Then she drove her point home, "Now I have about had it. I'm sorry if you are upset but I will NOT tolerate this behavior from you. Now you go and apologize to Ruth. Get your things and wait for me over there."

He didn't care. He had snapped.

He screamed, "NO! Leave me alone! I hate you and your stupid friends and this damn town!"

She barked, "Peter Zacchariah!"

He barked back, "Shut up!"

Funkle ran down the road.

Mom, mortified, walked back to Ruth while picking up hot-dogs.

She apologized, "Ruth. Oh my goodness. I am really sorry. It's not like him."

Sweet Ruth just consoled her, "Don't worry."

Mrs. F. confessed, "Listen I need to go."

Ruth assured her, "Go, go. I'll clean up. I'm sure he will be fine."

Mrs. F. responded, "Thanks, Ruth."

She gathered her things.

Almost at the end of the road, Peter was clear out of breath from running so he stopped. Still raging, he cried.

Suddenly, Sally came running up behind him.

She whispered gently, "Hey Peter. Peter."

He turned around to see her and quickly turned back picking up speed.

Funkle exploded, "Sally-Anne, go away. Did I tell you to follow me home?"

Shocked, she politely replied, "I didn't Peter. I live up this way. Hey don't worry about those jerks, OK?"

He couldn't contain his anger, "Shut up! I don't even know why you're talking to me. Who said I was worried? Leave me alone."

She was losing her patience by now, "Peter, but I thought we were going to play music together and stuff."

He took his anger out on her, "Yeah call me when you can really play!"

Then he ran off as fast as he could. Sally stopped, saddened by the comments of her first friend in town. Then a motorcycle zoomed driven by Mrs. Funkle. She noticed

Sally-Anne crying and stopped.

Mrs. F. approached the new girl, "Hey. Are you the girl that was with my son earlier?"

Sally-Anne obliged, "Yes, ma'am, with Peter, yes."

Mrs. F. pried, "Hey can you tell me what happened? Why are you crying? Why is my son acting nuts?"

Again she obliged this line of questioning, "Just some guys teasing Peter. Pete seemed so nice and now he's really being mean, kind of acting like a jerk, no disrespect to you Mrs. Funkle. But it kind of hurt my feelings. He was super sweet to me and I'm new here and all."

Mrs. F. answered Sally's pain with, "Yeah guys sometimes stink don't they? I'm sorry, sweetie. It really isn't like him to disrespect anyone this way. Do you need a lift home?"

Sally politely replied, "No, ma'am. I live in the blue house right there."

She pointed at the house.

Mrs. F. lightened up, "Oh did ya just move in?"

Peter was no longer in sight.

Sally answered, "Yeah. I don't know anyone, Pete was... well..."

Mrs. F. consoled her, "Well don't you worry, I'm going to straighten my son out. He doesn't usually act like...well, a jerk, frankly. Hey isn't your family going to watch the fireworks at the pond tonight?"

Sally smiled, "Yes I'm gonna get my dad and mom and hopefully we'll go back. Good night, Ma'am."

Sally-Anne sniffled as she walked into her house.

Mrs. F. took off on the bike with a mission.

Chapter Fourteen

Mrs. F. opened her front door with great force.

She hollered loud enough for people in Galilee to hear, "Peter Zaccariah Funkle, you get down here now. Yesterday isn't soon enough for me!"

The sound of a door slamming could be heard from upstairs. Suddenly Joan Baez music was blaring from the record player in Funkle's room.

Mrs. F. muttered to herself, "Joan Baez?!"

Then after a second she realized that it was her record.

She went ballistic, "That's my record! Turn that off or I'll give you something to sing a sad song over! Peter, lower that! And since when do you like Joan Baez?! Hello? Damn it Peter!"

Finally, she yanked her shoes off and threw them down one at a time as if preparing for a school-yard brawl. Mrs. F., on a mission, stormed up the stairs, an act which it seemed like lately, was becoming habitual. She wondered why her lovely boy was suddenly turning into a problem. Certainly, if she had consulted me about Funkle at the time, I could have shed insight. But obviously, she didn't.

Funkle turned up the volume even louder. The Baez concert played for the whole cul-de-sac, especially being that all the windows were open in the late summer heat.

I just have to add that if Funkle had this much gall with the evil boys, he never would've been tortured by us in the first place. That is not by any means an excuse for the events that ensued, but I truly believe we would have left him alone. And personally -- and I think even today Bobby would agree -- Mrs. F. was far scarier than any of us in my opinion.

Mrs. F. stormed back down the stairs. She had changed her mind deciding instead to give Pete his space. Then in a manic episode not unlike the ones familiar to mothers of teens everywhere, she turned back around and walked half way up the stairs again before once again turning around. Then as if she was prettying up for the arrival of company, Mrs. F. ran over to the TV, turned it on and plopped on the couch. She licked her fingers and patted her hair which was wildly messed up. Then she looked around as if she was on "Candid Camera."

The TV volume didn't drown out the music so she walked back over to the TV and turned it up as loud as possible. The entire neighborhood was being treated to TV laugh tracks mixed with a little Joan Baez.

The door bell rang several times as if someone was laying on it. Mrs. F. stood up and looked through the living room window from where she was standing. Then she mouthed to herself angrily, "PETER." She walked steadily over to the door but not before spitting once again on her fingers and patting down her frizzy hair.

Mrs. F. stood at the door, inhaled slowly, exhaled and then opened it to reveal Mrs. Bondi who lived across the street. She was the mom who was on the PTA and whose kids were the hall-monitors and eventually the local narcs. Nobody liked the old bag and we made it known. Every Halloween, her home was the house covered in the eggs and toilet paper.

Mrs. Bondi screamed her greeting so she could be heard over the music, "Mrs. Funkle?"

Nonchalantly, as if there was no issue, Mrs. F. smiled and shouted, "Mrs. Bondi?! Lovely to see you -- Happy Labor Day!"

Mrs. Bondi looked liked a typical commercial spokesperson in the 70s. She was a cross between Meredith Baxter Birney and Miss Piggy. She looked like Birney but sounded like Miss Piggy. Her husband Dan had won a settlement against the Ipswich police department years earlier when he was shot in the line of duty by a fellow cop who had gone rogue. So although the cops hated the Bondi family, the Bondi's were filthy rich. Years later, her son Joe was put away for racqueteering but the rumor was that he was set up. I wonder who could have done that?

Anyway, Mrs. Bondi didn't work and her husband owned a boat rental company. This gave them both plenty of time to be in everyone's business and they were. Mrs. B. stood there with one hand perched on her petite size 6 frame. She was wearing her predictable diamond pattern green-on-white, sleeveless, boat-neck mini-dress. Her pearls sat neatly and appropriately at the neckline. Her white heels stood at attention, one pointing to the right on a bent leg and one pointed directly ahead on a straight leg. Her blonde bouffant was tame in the humid air. How she had time to always mettle when she had six kids, no one could ever figure out.

Mrs. Bondi hollered angrily, "Mrs. Funkle. Good Day. Do

you realize that you are disturbing this lovely day for your neighbors? I have company and we can't even hear ourselves speak over the din. Can you please lower the music?! I implore you!"

Mrs. F. now had a purpose for her rage.

She let Mrs. Bondi have it, "Mrs. Bondi I have a teenager, I'm sure you can relate. He is slightly angry at the moment and he is choosing to use the volume of the music as a way of screaming at me. I'm sure you can remember when you were twelve or was it that long ago, now?"

Mrs. Bondi didn't take kindly to the age insult.

She warbled, "No, I cannot relate at all. My children behave and obey the rules of our household. Once again, there is no need to look beyond the parent for the answers to the child's unsettling behavior."

Mrs. F. was in rare form, "Ya know what, you are so right. There is no need to look beyond the parent for his unsettling behavior. In fact, how's this for unsettling?"

Mrs. F. used all her strength and the full length of her entire arm to yank back the door and return the door swinging with a giant slam shut in Bondi's face.

Then she said out loud to the closed door, "Good Day, Mrs. Bondi."

Mrs. F. had just about had it. She walked over to the couch and plopped herself down. Finally, out of frustration, she grabbed a couch pillow and buried her head under it. Ironically, the music turned off.

The next morning didn't alleviate the tension one bit.

Funkle sat at the table. He quietly rummaged through his cereal with his spoon, not eating much. The old, leather sax satchel, hung on his shoulder. Mrs. F., wearing only her bra and shorts, was visibly peeved. She opened the cabinet to get a glass. Then she slammed the glass onto the counter. She slammed the cabinet door shut. She opened the refrigerator to retrieve the orange juice. She poured it, put it back and slammed the refrigerator door shut. Angrily, she finally turned to address her son while she drank her juice.

First, she stared at him icily. Funkle didn't look away from his cereal bowl. It was safer. Almost to the bottom of the bowl, he dug in with his spoon repetitively, scooping up every last bit of milk to avoid her glare at any cost.

When he finished his breakfast, obviously frightened of his mother's fury, he still refused to look at her. Neither person moved or spoke. The rule in any game is the first one who speaks, loses.

And finally …

Mrs. F. yelled very loudly, "You're grounded!"

Funkle made a face at her loud tone.

Then he responded, "Got it."

She was determined to win this game he was playing, "Are you finished? Give me your bowl."

Funkle handed her the bowl, still refusing to look at her.

She was getting madder. She upped the ante, "OK, get a scrub brush and start with the bathroom."

He didn't move.

Finally, enraged, she barked, "Peter, take that bag off of

your shoulder and MOVE!"

Still, he had no response.

She countered, "Peter!"

Then luckily for Funkle, the phone rang. She turned away to answer it.

Mrs. F. in her phone voice spoke like a stewardess, "Hello. Yes. This is. Oh. Hi. How are you doing--"

Then he did it. In an act of ultimate defiance and against Mrs. F. of all people, Funkle ran out choosing to completely ignore his grounded status.

Mrs. F. muted the phone by covering the mouth-piece with her boob.

She hollered, "Peter!"

The front door slammed behind him.

She screamed louder, "Peter!"

Then she frantically resumed her conversation putting the handset back up to her ear, "Ruth, I gotta call you back."

She hung up and ran out of the front door to catch her son.

Chapter Fifteen

Peter huffed and puffed as he walked briskly away from his house. The leather pouch kept hitting his belly as he trudged along. He had hoped his mom would choose not to follow him. So far she wasn't too brutal, even with all the testing he had been doing.

Mrs. F. snuck up behind Peter. The smell of grilled burgers coming from someone's yard, she was sentimental and wanted to stop this awful rage that was taking over her son. He was her only family. She was about to stop him and give him a huge punishment when she saw Sally-Anne meet and greet Peter. They walked off, her uneven pig-tails bouncing against the back of her purple tie-dye T-shirt. The long hippie beads that hung from her macramé vest -- which resembled a knotted plant holder --whistled in the summer wind as she walked.

Mrs. F. wanted badly to confront him but she chose at the last minute to let him go. He never even saw her behind him. When I think about it, I'm not sure a mother in her situation would have acted any differently. Here was this kid who was ostracized, fat, smelled at times and was painfully shy and now a girl was actually paying attention to him. What mother would not have had at least some compassion and a little bit of admiration at the reason for his act of defiance, his crush on this girl. What mother wouldn't act that way? I pause a moment to ponder the irony of my own question. Since I can only conjecture what my wife might do now for our son. My mother certainly would never have shown that kind of mettle in order to protect my well-being or would have had any compassion for my precious life. So I don't speak from a place of knowing. Even her death was selfishly motivated. But I can certainly watch children of single mothers in my practice who would give their lives for their children's happiness. And I know my wife would certainly have allowed our son a free pass that day. Funkle was so lucky in many ways and so unlucky in many others.

So on that muggy day after the fair, Pete and Sally-Anne walked hand-in-hand savoring the newness. The air was so thick that summer. It was the kind of humidity that makes you yearn for a shower as soon as you step outside the door. The heavy air seemed to foreshadow fate's plans for all of us.

Peter stopped abruptly.

In a distrustful voice, he intoned, "Did the guys put you up to this?"

Confused, Sally-Anne responded, "Pardon?"

One can't really blame the big lug for his developing paranoia. I mean we did have something up our sleeves at every turn and it always involved Funkle Fattie.

He insisted, "The guys!"

Sally-Anne answered as if she was spelling a letter at the local spelling bee, "I'm sorry. Define. What is the source of this?"

He continued, "Did they dare you? To pretend you dig me?"

She laughed at him, "You really are an odd duck Peter. Why would you think that? I mean, I dig you. It's no big secret. Has no girl ever wanted you to ask her to go steady before?"

Then Sally-Anne blushed realizing that she had revealed too much. She pushed her coke-bottle eye glasses up the freckled bridge of her nose.

Peter cleared his throat, "Steady? Oh. I guess that's OK. But I'm a fat guy, Sally."

She laughed, "So we are, um, steady? Anyway, I'm tall silly, so what. And besides, you're tall too. You carry it well. You're silly is what! And you're my steady boyfriend!"

He looked at her speechless for a moment, partly because he didn't know how she suddenly became his girlfriend and partly because he had no answers. Then she squeezed his hand so hard that orange juice was practically coming out of it.

He couldn't help blurt out, "Ouch."

She planted a huge kiss on his lips.

Funkle thought he probably didn't like all the metal that kind of got caught on everything, but he didn't hate the kiss either.

He hugged her tightly.

Then he peered into her lenses which eventually led to her eyes behind all that glass. She was mesmerized by his baby blues and before anyone could say Funkle Fattie, they made out for the first time.   Rumor was that he had an erection for weeks after that. Waldo said Mrs. Bondi had asked him to take care of his little "person" with discretion, please (her words). Because his wanker just wouldn't go down in his too-tight khakis. It just kept standing at attention. Of course I never looked down. I would've been called a sis by the guys so I just took their word for it. I kind of thought silently though it was a good thing for him. I figured the big lug deserved a good woody after all we had put him through. Again, I never shared this empathic line of thinking with any of my comrades. They would've somehow converted it to:

"Gross, Greeney jerks off thinking about Funkle's wood. Sick!"

I was sure of it. So I only secretly cheered him on.

When the make-out session ended, he took Sally's hand. They walked away, cooing. And then Peter wiped the pink Baby Girl lip gloss off his lips onto his shoulder staining his new short sleeve shirt from Woolworth's. Again, what is it they say about Rome not being built in a day? Truer words were never spoken.

Funkle and Sally-Anne walked home, the memory of their first make-out session together, still fresh. He pulled out some icing-filled cookies from his knapsack, handed her one -- a big show of affection on his part, sharing food -- and they walked off. As Sally-Anne nibbled on her cookie, black Oreo crumbs were getting stuck in her dental work, but she hadn't a care in the world. Her smile was bigger than ever.

Then as with every precious moment in Funkle Fattie's life, I rode up to destroy it. My Huffy bad boy skidded to a stop right in front of Sally, cutting them both off.

Sally-Anne jumped back with a big thump on her wooden clogs.

Funkle stepped up to say, "Go away, Greeney. I'm not buggin' ya. Go away."

I had to play my cards right or I would never be able to heal my Gramps.

Shyly I muttered in my high voice that was beginning to crack from impending puberty, "Awe geez, Pete. I don't want no trouble. I told ya, we could be best buddies now. Bygones and all that--"

Peter answered reluctantly as he spit out an Oreo piece upon speaking, "OK. Well can't you see, I'm busy with my girl?"

I crackled, "Yeah, I see."

And then as much as it killed me because I really just didn't like the sight of her, I extended my pudgy, freckled hand out toward Sally-Anne.

Then I spoke painfully, "Tommy Greene's the name. Live over by the tracks. Nice ta meetcha. Any good frienda Funkle's must be groovy. So yeah--um, nice meetin' ya."

It just killed me to be that cordial. And her hand not only dwarfed mine but it was so sweaty. I still cringe when I think about that silly, most painful of introductions.

As she sized me up, I coyly wiped my hand on my Red Sox shirt. Then I wiped it some more on my green corduroy shorts.

Sally-Anne hesitated. Clearly she had been a little more street-wise than Funkle in his day.

She finally answered, "Sally-Anne Gregor."

I kind of stood there stunned for a moment because I was

trying to figure out what the black in her teeth was. Then it occurred to me that it was Oreo residue. I was close to nausea by this point.

Suddenly in a move fit for Bobby Orr, Sally and Funkle tried to pass me like I was a puck. But I was having none of it. I squared my bad boy, my black and Silver Huffy to block them. They were mine.

I took my moment, "So Pete...OK if I call ya Pete?

He didn't answer.

I continued, "So Pete, now that we are pals, wanna come over to my house tomorrow?"

Funkle nodded, "Nah."

Then Sally-Anne put in her two cents. She was very quickly becoming a huge obstacle in my plan.

She giggled as she spoke and spit, "Mr. Funkle and I have a date."

I couldn't contain myself.

Sarcastically, I came back with, "Far out. Breaking news, Pete's got a girl."

Then I had to pull it back and win them over so I asked very sincerely, "Well, swell you can come to."

Sally-Anne answered cheerily, "Oh. Well, sure, I guess. Pete?"

Peter grumbled, "Nah."

Then I just pleaded, "My Gramps would really dig your playin'. He loves music more than most anything! Can't you guys just make your date at my house?"

Sally-Anne inquired, "Oh, does he play too?

I almost cried, "Naw. He's real sick. Real sick--"

Sally-Anne showed her concern in her hippie way, "Oh. Oh wow, sorry. That's deep, sorry Tommy. Really deep, heavy! Pete, whad-ya say?! We probably oughta go, huh?"

Funkle wasn't buying any of it. He just appeased her.

In a monotone voice, he whispered, "Yeah maybe, sure. We really gotta go now, Tommy."

Then he pushed his way past my bike. But I insisted on driving the point home in case they hadn't really meant to agree to come over.

Eagerly, I hollered, "Well, groovy. See ya tomorrow. Yeah-- and you too Sally. Don't forget the flute, uh, uh I mean saxophone. Thanks Pete, buddy."

It wasn't exactly a winning moment for me. It only made me feel more ashamed of who I was. But that was the problem that my twelve year old mind grappled with. I wasn't anyone without my gramps. I couldn't see my way past the pain. The third abandonment in my young life, loomed large. And this one mattered. He really cared for me. My parents never did. Desperation was causing me all kinds of confusion. It could only get worse.

Chapter Sixteen

I saw that the evil boys were riding up to join me. Carrie rode side-saddle on Kenny's bike and you could see her Super Girl underwear under her yellow mini-dress. She wore ugly, green leather sandals that had beige yarn woven into the wedge of the rubber-soled heels. Her black long hair was adorned with a daisy which held it half back. And her tiny, perky breasts were nearly peeking out of the V neck. She had a pack of Camels tucked under the ankle strap of her shoe. The sight of Carrie with all of her bad-girl tendencies, heightened my own keen awareness of my duplicitous behavior. The lies I had told Sally-Anne who was so innocent and quite the opposite of Carrie. I didn't know whether to feel jealous that Kenny dated the cute, neighborhood tramp or mad that I had to spend time with Sally-Anne or just angry at myself and my situation in general. Maybe I felt all of the above. I couldn't handle it so I spit a giant ball of phlegm and peeled off in the other direction. As I met up with the slow pokes, I made sure to let Sally and Pete walk past my bike safely before the boys could stop them or get a look at them.

But Waldo and Kenny noticed Sally and Pete right away. Kenny was really fuming that I had done nothing but block the guys from Fattie. They stared at me as I stopped to inevitably greet my "friends."

Bobby must have gotten a tan at the picnic. His face was so brown and his hair was so blonde. He looked like he should have been playing tennis in Malibu. He wore his classic, very, white tennis shoes, a white tennis shirt which was adorned with red, white and blue stripes at the end of each short sleeve and short red canvas shorts. He just didn't belong in Ipswich.

I barked at them, "What?"

Kenny answered, "I think you're a sissy who likes blubber fat boys."

Suddenly, I noticed that he had a big scratch above his eye. I felt a momentary sense of satisfaction because I think I had given that to him in the scuffle we had at the fair. Well there I thought, was my in.

I laughed, "Shut up before I sock you and knock your lights out. Hey, bad scratch you got there on your eye, huh? Did I give that to ya? Sorry, man"

Kenny sucker punched me in the stomach. Bobby started laughing in that crazy way that he always did. He acknowledged that I'd scored big-time with my come-back comment. Then I tackled Kenny and we start fighting. What else do boys do when there are no more words? They talk about girls or fight it out.

I got in a really good punch to his gut. Kenny spit up a little dirt on his white T-shirt.

Waldo screamed, "Kenny don't be a wimp, man!"

Waldo picked his nose and threw the dry snot on the ground.

Then he resumed, "Kick his sorry ass, Kenny."

Bobby joined in, "Shut up Waldo 'fore I kick your extra tooth from here to Michigan."

Waldo didn't respond. I think he was probably trying to figure out where Michigan was. He's probably still trying to figure it out.

I got in one last good punch to Kenny's side and then he kicked me in the groin, hard. I crumpled onto the ground groaning. I wondered for a moment if those kicks were as painful for Funkle. And then I thought that Kenny probably kicked Funkle twice as hard. That had to hurt.

Kenny razzed me, "Greeney, I never took you for no sis-boy."

Waldo repeated unoriginally, "Sissy!"

The boys skidded away.

I was close to tears but there was no way I was going to let it happen. I got up clutching my side. I kicked the ground, spit and cursed as much as I could.

I screamed almost hoping they could hear me, "Fuckers. Shit-for-brains. I just want that damn flute. Fuck-holes."

****

Peter was on his knees, scrubbing the toilet at the Funkle residence. He was dripping sweat. Sally-Anne washed the mirror and occasionally she would grab a tissue and dab Pete's forehead. Joan Baez music played softly in the background while Sally-Anne hummed to it and mouthed the words.

Mrs. F. entered. She was particularly dolled up in a long, yellow, terry-cloth maxi-dress that tied like a halter at her neck. Her hair was pulled tightly back into a bun. She munched on grapes, a healthy treat as opposed to her usual chips or Mac 'N Cheese. Maybe she was trying to shed her bad-ass image in the same way Funkle was trying to shed his blubber image. Mrs. Bondi said at the time that there were very few times she had witnessed Mrs. F. wearing a dress. Bondi swore that one of those times was when she had noticed Mrs. F. in the car in a very lusty liaison with Coach Wilson. And the other time was right after Mrs. B had admonished Mrs. F. for her son's loud music. And of course we all knew that Bondi knew everything about everybody.

Mrs. F. spoke out of the side of her grape-filled mouth, "It better be spotless! Peter, YOU had better make that bathroom sparkle."

Sally-Anne answered for her sweetie, "We are! I mean, he is Mrs. Funkle."

Then she turned to address Pete, "So think about it OK?"

Peter answered Sally, "Maybe."

She continued, sweetly, "With his Grandpa being sick, he may have changed is all."

Pete laughed, "Yeah, right. I heard."

Mrs. F. interrupted, "Peter, at this rate you'll be havin' Christmas dinner by the toilet."

Mrs. F. winked at Sally-Anne and exited.

Pete scrubbed harder.

Sally-Anne added, "Your mom's cool."

Pete, a man of few words muttered, "Yep."

Chapter Seventeen

Sally and Pete walked toward my house. They were acting naively in an attempt by Sally to trust my word. They passed a few boarded up, dilapidated homes and then a liquor store until they hit the tracks. They were about twenty yards away when Sally-Anne noticed me standing in the distance. I was just outside of my house, smoking. I looked down at the ground and kicked imaginary dirt around with each slow inhale.

Finally I spotted Funkle. I don't know if his girl was dressing him already but he had on these made-for-skinny-guys low-waist beige corduroys that looked ridiculous with his stomach hanging out. And he wore hippie, Jesus-sandals and a purple buttoned down, short-sleeve polyester shirt that you might catch on Burt Reynolds. He had it open to the third button. And he wore a hand-beaded necklace. It was ridiculous. I couldn't help but notice the huge rounded sweat ponds under each of his arm pits. His hair was parted on the side and hung in his face.

Sally-Anne wore a pink sun-dress with yellow flowers all over it. Again the sickly sweet sight of her made me throw up a little in my mouth. But I guess this was my pay-back because I couldn't make fun of Fattie even though I was so ready to.

There was an awkward silence. Sally, of course could be counted on to break the ice. She didn't disappoint.

She shouted in my direction, "Hi Tommy."

I stared at her and then cracked a bit of a smile. Suddenly, unbeknownst to them as it was only visible in my line of vision, I saw them. My smile turned to fright.

Carrie and Kenny were playfully chasing each other in the distance behind Sally and Peter as they approached my neck of the woods. They were clearly unaware of any of us at the moment. But this meant, I would have to cover. They couldn't know about this plan to hang out together. Kenny would ruin me for sure.

Then Sally broke the silence again unfortunately for me. This time Kenny turned when he heard Sally's voice and Carrie stopped in her tracks. I couldn't help notice Carrie. She was so cute in her short denim cut-off shorts and candy-cane striped halter top. I wanted her badly. But I didn't have time to indulge my fantasy life, I had to act quickly.

Sally-Anne was determined to destroy me with her stupid blather, "Hey Tommy, Pete brought the saxello to play for your gramps and I even brought my guitar. We can have like a jam session."

Kenny stamped out a cigarette and looked at me through a squint that said, "I'm onto you."

I was fucked.

Sally-Anne turned around, stunned. She turned back to look for a reaction from Tommy that would signal I was on the right team. I didn't give her any. She looked at Pete and you could tell now that they both thought that I had set them up.

Kenny walked in between Tommy and Pete. Then he

walked up to Carrie and kissed her. She giggled.

He swaggered as he spoke, "Carrie, Skunka Chunka here came to play for my sis boy, Greeney."

Carrie laughed.

Kenny completed his thought, "Carrie, tell Greene that we don't hang out with blubber, sissy boys."

Carrie shouted over to me, "Tommy are you a sis? 'Cuz you're sure actin' like it lately."

I wanted to shout out, "No, Carrie. I just jerked off to the thought of you in that mini-dress!"

But Kenny would have knocked all of my teeth out so I didn't say it.

Instead I just covered for myself by saying, "Naw. Mind your own beeswax, butt-hole. I ain't doin' nothin' but standin' here smokin' at my own home. And then all of a sudden Skunka-Funka says he's come to play for me. Eeeiow, you gotta crush on me Funkle? Man, he's a wicked sissy, you guys. It ain't me for nothin'!"

I laughed as hard as I could, over compensating for my obvious untruth.

Sally's mouth was so wide open, you could drive a truck though it.

After she gathered herself, she spoke up, "We came to play 'cuz YOU said--"

I had to stop her. My life was at stake.

I growled, "Zip your lip four-eyes!"

Peter became enraged at that comment. He got in the football stance that Coach had taught him and charged

Kenny as hard as he could. He toppled him and then started for me.

Sally-Anne screamed, "No Pete stop! You mean guys. Go away! We brought the sax for you Tommy and you know it!"

Kenny still on the ground, pulled at Peter's polyester shirt and ripped some of the buttons off. Now Pete's belly was hanging out. He got up embarrassed.

Then he whispered, out of breath to Sally, "Sally-Anne, c'mon."

Kenny mocked her, "But Tommy, they brought the flute!!"

Then Kenny committed the ultimate sin of the day. He grabbed the sax out of Pete's bag. He mimicked playing. Carrie laughed. Then she pretended to dance. Sally-Anne kicked Kenny in the groin. He doubled over moaning. Carrie lunged hard for Sally-Anne.

Sally-Anne pointed to Carrie's chin.

She said, "Hey look Carrie, you have a giant pimple on your chin! Oh my goodness, it's oozing!"

Carrie, not too bright, looked down, panicked which gave Sally the opportunity to aggressively snap Carrie's bra. Sally pulled Peter by the hand and they started running.

Kenny and Carrie walked off with Pete's sax.

Sally-Anne screamed back at me, "You oughta be ashamed of yourself. If anyone is a sissy, I think it's you."

I couldn't take it any more. I ran after Kenny and Carrie.

I pleaded, "C'mon, give it Kenny! You ain't gonna play it."

Kenny laughed at me.

Then I warned him, "Give it or I tell Carrie about the rash

on your--"

Kenny shut me up before I could say it.

He exploded with, "Shut up pea-for-brains."

He threw the sax at me.

I yelled at them, "Now get outta here. I don't got time for your crap!"

They finally left. Kenny kicked the dirt in my direction.
I ran to catch up to Pete and Sally.

I pleaded again, "Guys wait please. My grandpa could really use some music. PLEASE!"

Pete and Sally looked at each other. Sally nodded in approval.

Pete reluctantly grabbed his sax and followed me inside. Again, had I stopped to notice the kind nature of this kid, my actions would have maybe been different. I would have never given the likes of me another chance no matter what the situation was. But I was blinded by my mission.

Pete and Sally waited awkwardly in the living room. Peter nervously pulled the unraveled thread from the green velvet sofa. Sally-Anne pointed to the velvet Elvis paintings on the wall. No sooner did she see that but she pointed to the oxygen tank near my Gramps' bedroom. Peter just kind of looked away. It freaked him out a little. He reached over to grab her sweaty hand.

I walked gingerly toward my bed-ridden grandfather's room as I quietly cried. I walked into my Gramps' bedroom, the whole time keeping my eyes tightly closed. Carefully I approached his bedside. I could smell orange peels for some reason.

I said these words exactly as I ran into the room, "Gramps, just hold on. I'm gonna get you healed quick, I swear! I promise. I promised Jesus last night that I would give up my bike and smokin' if he could get me that sax to heal you. And he did, Gramps. He did."

Then I opened my eyes wide to face my sickly grandfather and was shocked by the sight of an empty bed.

I ran around the house panicked, looking for him. Then I ran straight into the chest of the chaplain.

The chaplain...now there was a great man. He was tall with a big barrel chest and he always smelled like potpourri. I only remember his white priest collar back then because it seemed I was always looking up at him. He had silver, very tiny spectacles and very neatly parted black hair with speckles of gray. His lips were always pink from his addiction to lip balm. He was probably six and half feet tall. Using the phrase 'good man' to describe him would be like calling Mother Theresa a fairly nice lady.

I wailed, "Where's Gramps?"

The chaplain responded calmly, "In the bath son. The nurse is bathing him. He was well enough to sit up today."

I cheered, "That's great!! He's getting better! He'll be better in no time!"

The chaplain braced himself, "He's well enough to bathe son, that's all. He's well enough to bathe."

I ignored him.

"Right, well my friend's gonna play his healin' songs for him today so we'll just wait, OK?"

He whispered to me, "Son, I don't think it's a ---"

Undeterred, I countered, "We'll wait in the living room."

And we did. Peter, Sally Anne and I waited in the living room for what seemed like an eternity. It was the longest I'd ever spent with Peter without teasing him. He wasn't so bad actually. He had a whole bag of cookies that he shared and he had more knock-knock jokes stored in his memory than any guy I knew. And they were funny. In my mind, when it became so satiated with painful, frightening thoughts of losing my grandpa, I would drift off and silently form a strategy of how I could maybe, possibly -- and I was only entertaining the notion --- become friends with Pete without the other guys knowing. Then reality would hit and I would remind myself of the impossibility of that crazy notion.

The air was filled with the heaviness of enforced silence. It was the kind of silence that people resort to because saying something, even the smallest thing, is a reminder of the seriousness of the moment. So nobody dared to speak. My new-found friends were visibly uncomfortable. Peter had practically eaten his nails down to the quick. And if that weren't visible evidence of his nerves, the sweat stains on the couch cushions were. It wasn't that hot in the house. But I wasn't about to let them go. Sally, of course, kept smiling through it all.

So we waited. Finally Sally-Anne turned to Peter, cupping his ear as she whispered. I was hoping she was whispering sweet-nothings into his ear but I knew she really just wanted to politely excuse herself.

Peter laughed at whatever Sally had whispered and then spoke up, "Hey Tommy, I really have to get going. Hope your Grandpa feels better."

The chaplain entered giving the couple another out. He braced his spectacles on his nose and spoke in a very metered tone. He sounded like a cross between Robert Kennedy and Donny Osmond. The endings of his sentences always ended on an up-note like Osmond but he had that classic Kennedy accent and metered, quick way of speaking. And he even resembled Joseph Kennedy.

"Hey Tom, son, Gramps needs to get some sleep now. Maybe you could ask your guests to come again another day."

Sally-Anne jumped at the notion of freedom, "Yep. We were just goin', right Pete?"

Peter smiled, "Uh, yeah."

The chaplain escorted them out. Sally-Anne's hippie beads made noise all the way out to the walk-way. The chaplain smiled at me with that look that even as a child you know forewarns of sad news.

"Son, your Grandpa is not doing..."

I interrupted rudely. I was too frightened to hear the truth.

"Yeah it's great isn't? He is sittin' up now. He'll be singin' "Danny Boy" soon enough like he use ta!!

I ran away defiantly. And then for some reason, I think because I couldn't contain my anger, I started singing and screaming "Danny Boy."

"Oh Danny Boy, the pipes, the pipes..."

Peter and Sally-Anne walked home. The smell of summer mixed with sweat lingered on them. Peter really didn't notice that he smelled musty because he was intoxicated by Sally-Anne's scent which was an odd combination of coconut skin cream and strawberry flavored lip gloss. Sally-Anne adjusted the giant guitar on her shoulder so she could lean in to kiss Peter on the cheek.

Suddenly the mood turned serious.

Peter confided, "I told you."

And he pulled out some salt water taffy to share.

She handed it back.

She explained, "It gets stuck in my braces really badly. What did you tell me?"

He put it back his bag and handed her some chocolate chip cookies. She took them and munched.

He continued, the blow softened by the gift of cookies, "I told you. I warned you that Tommy was a jerk. Next time let me fight my own battles, 'K? Guys have 'ta fight their own battles," Pete insisted.

She smiled gently, "Sure Peter. Your rhetoric is so ancient history. I'm a modern woman. I read 'Cosmo,' ya know?"

Pete look baffled as he uttered, "Huh? 'Cosmo.' Anyway, awe gee, I'm just saying. Just leave the guy stuff to me, 'K?"

She agreed, "Alright. You're pretty groovy, know that?"

He blushed and muttered, "Yeah, groovy."

Pete and Sally-Anne arrived at Pete's house. He seemed kind of relieved. Between all the issues with Tommy's grandfather and Sally-Anne being all over him, he just needed a dose of TV and a bowl of Mac N' Cheese. A guy's gotta have his guy time. Well he knew she'd probably join but he planned to zone out a little. He had a lot on his twelve year old mind. Sally-Anne kissed him with a small peck to the cheek and they went inside.

Chapter Eighteen

While summer wasn't over in our minds, a new academic year was upon us. Some of us did quite a bit of growing up, myself excluded, over the three months. Peter and Sally-Anne were young love-birds and he had found a new heir of confidence, although that didn't stop us from resuming the bullying where we had left off.

Peter and Sally-Anne exited the school laughing. Trailing behind them was a skinny guy whose face was speckled with acne. He was nameless although I could pick him out of the yearbook. Behind him was a guy with curly black hair and a jaw harness, and just behind them were Funkle's new friends Benny who was an all-around goof ball and Lucy. She had hair that was so frizzy, it arrived before she did. It was like a nest, sandy brown and a complete wiry bowl of frizz. It had none of the usual sheen that young hair has. Benny was a nice guy, though. We never really made fun of him even though he was very odd looking. He had a huge nose that made a bunch of twists and turns before ending at his puffy, chapped lips. He also had strange eye lids that were unusually droopy. He could always be found making some corny joke or being dared to do something totally stupid. As the misfits exited, they passed me and Kenny and Waldo. Funkle and all of us guys were not in the same grade any more because he had skipped to ninth grade. However we were still on the same campus. We had ditched the first day so we could smoke and raise hell instead. Kenny hucked spitballs aimed right at Peter's face. One hit Funkle but he ignored it. The second one hit Coach Wilson who had stopped right in front of Peter to obviously tell him something.

The Coach saw where it came from and he took off after Kenny. I turned and ran the other way. I was laughing so hard I nearly peed. Funkle and his friends just walked off hardly affected. The balance was beginning to shift here and I wasn't sure I liked it. This new Peter was getting on my nerves.

****

Mrs. F., Peter and Sally shared conversation over dinner that evening.

Mrs. F. approached the subject gently, "So, Coach Wilson says try-outs for the team are soon and he'd like you --"

Peter interrupted with his normal lack of enthusiasm, "Yeah. I don't think so."

Sally-Anne always got her two bits in, "It's a very violent game, isn't it, Peter?"

Peter just ignored it all, "Can you pass the tuna?"

Mrs. F. continued, "Pete, I think you should at least think about it."

Clearly not interested, Peter agreed anyway. "Fine. Mom, did you bring home Whoopie pies?"

Mrs. F. was not happy with the tactic her son was taking, "Peter! Why are you ignoring me?"

Finally he answered directly, "I'm a musician, not a jock, Mom. I play music not sports."

She gave him a typical maternal answer, "Maybe you could

do both."

He gave her a typical teenage answer, "Dunno. So did you bring home Whoopie pies?"

Mrs. F. conceded the loss. She pulled the wrapped dessert out of a bag and threw it at Peter.

Peter reacted, "Ouch!"

Funkle stood on the football field dressed in football padding and a jersey amongst a line-up of guys, all different sizes but most of whom looked athletic. The word was that Funkle looked like a meatball in a jersey. At least that is what Kenny's brother, told Kenny, who told us. He was quite large for his age and that was apparent as he lined up next to his peers. He had one goal. He was there to try out at the request of his mother and the urging of Coach Wilson. But Funkle had figured that it would be a simple act of compliance that would lead to his display of sucking at football. And then he would be victorious. The talk of sports would be finished. So he did nothing to prepare and read nothing about the rules of a game which he could care less about.

We watched try-outs from the bleachers -- high up in the nose bleeds so we could smoke and sneak beers. Bobby was actually into it and cheered on some of the guys. It was so obvious to the outside world that Bobby was selling himself short being our friend, even we recognized it. But none of us were going to reveal that.

Peter ran down the field pushing a moving barrier. He grunted and I think I even heard him fart a couple of times.

He was actually pretty good... at the game that is. We have already established that he had a gift for the art of the fart. The coach took notes and blew his whistle incessantly. I wanted to rip it off his neck but then he would've ripped me a new set of family jewels so I behaved. Stan, Kenny's brother, a big high-school football star, was all over Funkle.

Coach screamed at him, "Hey Stan, show 'em how it's done."

Stan brutalized the rolling, bean-stuffed bag. The young tryouts looked terrified. Then Stan walked up to Funkle after he was finished.

He spoke in a raspy tone, "Hey are you my brother Kenny's friend?"

Funkle nodded and answered, "No."

Stan pushed, "Yeah you're the sissy kid who crapped in his pants. He said he caught you tryin' to make the moves on Tommy."

Funkle gulped, "No way."

Stan laughed. "Awe man, you better be careful. There ain't no room for flute-playin', sissy, football players on this team."

Stan pulled up Funkle's sweats which gave Pete a mean wedgy. Then in an act of pure reaction, Funkle kneed him in the groin.

Kenny yelled from the stands, "Awe shit, Stan, kick his fat ass!"

Coach Wilson pointed directly at Kenny as if to say, if you don't shut up, I am going to get you. Kenny cowered.

But in the shocker of all-time shocking-est school memories, Funkle made the team. We were steamed, real hot under the collar! Bobby however, silently at least, probably thought it was kind of cool.

It went down like this. Funkle and the boy with the jaw harness who has never been given a name, Benny, Lucy, and Sally-Anne as well as other athletes gathered around the posting outside of the athletic office. Some, after reading the print-out would run away excited and some others were visibly disappointed. I was on punishment that day for peeing on the side of the school so I was ordered to clean out the bathroom stalls which were right by the athletic office. I spied. I was very anticipatory and very much hoping that this wouldn't be a favorable outcome for Funkle's football career. Namely, my first reason for wanting Funkle to NOT make the team was that I didn't want him to lose interest in playing the healing sax because Gramps had a very short time to live and I needed him to play it for him. But selfishly, the second reason was that I didn't want the pecking order to change at all.

Funkle stood back from the board. He didn't even look.

Sally-Anne, of course acted like the cheerleader even though she looked nothing like one.

She chirped, "Aren't you gonna look?"

Eavesdropping, I threw up a little in my mouth -- just my normal reaction to syrupy-sweet Sally.

Funkle chirped back, "Naw."

She pushed him, "What's wrong? You liked it! Gosh you

can play music and sports too ya know, like your mom said! Oh Lord."

Goofball Benny interjected, "Why are we here then?"

Funkle retorted, "Who asked you?"

Benny responded affably, "True. Hey let's go get egg malts at Fred Derby's, then."

Funkle didn't move.

Sally sensed that he really did want to know and took charge as she spoke, "Oh good golly. You must want to see."

She pushed through the crowd of big jocks.

I rolled my eyes. Then quite accidentally, a giant burp slipped out. Lucy heard it and turned to notice me spying on the players. Flirting, I winked at her and put my finger up to my mouth as if to say, sssh. She giggled like a little girl and complied. Thank God for ugly girls, I thought to myself.

Sally barked, "Scuse me. Pardon me. Scuse me. Thank you."

She tilted her head up to read the roster. Then she looked visibly confused.

Sally leaned in to ask another player, "Um, scuse me."

She politely tapped the player who happened to be standing next to her.

She asked him, "'Scuse me? Does Starting LB/Tight End mean you are on the team? That's good right? Checkin' for my boyfriend--"

Sally pointed to the letters next to Funkle's name on the roster.

The guy answered, annoyed, "Yeah. That's good. That's good, alright … Girls!"

The player looked as if he indeed had probably not made it onto the team. He showered Sally-Anne and Pete with an icy glare and walked away.

Sally-Anne hollered back to her friends, "So Pete, you are LB/Tight End and first string. Benny, Lucy, now we can go to Fred Derby's."

They all cheered including Pete. And yes he was becoming more and more Pete, less and less Funkle Fattie, at least to me.

The odd group rolled away. They cheered and joked. I returned to the bathroom stalls to complete my detention. Lucy waved at me and winked.

Needless to say, I was devastated. Somehow I knew this could end my dream of getting Pete to heal my Grandfather. Desperation kicked in. All I can actually recall about the rest of that day was scrubbing the stalls as hard as I could with my little hands and a tooth-brush in an attempt to get my anger out. It didn't work.

Peter knew that being a part of a winning football team, could potentially increase his popularity. So of course he agreed to play. He was no fool.

Kenny and the guys thought it was only a matter of time before Pete blew it. They had no intention of letting up on him. Kenny even suggested that Stan would make sure the team would make it a living hell for Pete. My private opinion: Stan didn't give two licks about his family or his little brother Kenny or their alcoholic parents. Kenny's thesis, in my mind, was garbage. I knew enough to know that performance on a team out-weighs physique, bad skin or a bad case of gas. But I would have gotten my ass kicked if I revealed this revelation. So I didn't.

Chapter Nineteen

Over the next few days of practice, Peter became the talk
of the school. Those who hated him were talking about his
new stint as a football player. Those who had never heard of
him were chatting about this new fat phenom who was sure
to take us to victory.

Funkle was learning about football, although he still wasn't
completely comfortable with his teammates. At one
particular practice, Peter stood on the football field ready to
do battle. He wore a blue jersey, Stan wore red. Peter took
the center position and faced Stan. The thing that made
Peter so good was that he was completely unaware that this
was a game, for him it was war. And the rumor was, at least
according to Stan, that Pete would grunt or yell the words
Waldo or Kenny before making a play.

Anyway on this particular day, after the snap of the ball, he
pulverized Stan. When the play was over, the coach came
over to help Stan back up. Coach was notably impressed. I
watched with Kenny who made us guys go to practice every
day. I think he was obsessed. This day I looked over at
Kenny to view his reaction at Stan's pulverization. He was
blushing from ear to ear. I laughed and pointed at Kenny.
He threw his cap at me. This just didn't look good for any of
us.

Peter snapped out of his anger and walked over to the
coach to rub it in.

He said in an atypically loud voice, "Ooh. Uh, sorry, Coach.
Is Stan alright?"

The coach wasn't about to tolerate showboating on either party's part.

He warned Pete, "Ssh. Zip it. Just do what ya do and leave Stan out of it. He's a senior. And you ain't nothin' but a, wet behind the ears, magnet school, eighth grader. Don't get cocky, son. But,nicely done!"

Later in the locker room, according to rampant rumors, Stan was walking like a duck, like he was in pain, like maybe he had a rod up his rear-end. One of the cool, team-player-type guys, Joe Winston, approached Pete. He patted him on the back.

Joe smiled at him as he spoke, "Hey guy. You got some smooth moves for a rookie. Right on."

Peter smiled from ear to ear.

The coach addressed the team, "We got work to do guys but I'm proud of every last one of you. Keep it up. Oh and by the way, nice work, Pete."

The coach sauntered out. All the guys crowded in one spot for the showers. None of the guys paid any attention to the fact that most of them were naked. But Peter who was shielded by the locker embankment, was acutely aware of Stan watching him. He knew this was a make or break moment. He absolutely felt Stan about to make fun of him after he disrobed.

At first, Peter stalled by digging through his equipment bag. Then in a desperate attempt to avoid the ridicule, when no one was looking, he farted deliberately. He followed the blast with hollers and disgusted looks to call attention to

Stan for the amusement of the other guys. Then he moved away so the guys would track the smell directly to Stan.

Finally Pete took one last risk with these words, "Awe shit, Stan. Damn. What did you have for breakfast? Man! I gotta get outta here."

He ran out, still dressed in his football uniform.

Stan, who was still stuck standing there, looked at the other guys who were clearly gassed out by the smell.

He down played it, "C'mon. I didn't cut the cheese. It was lard-ass."

Obviously, no one believed Stan. The players just stared and laughed at him.

Stan recouped, "Yeah OK, ass-holes. Go clean off your sorry behinds."

Moments later, Peter met Benny outside of the athletic office.

He pulled Benny aside and confided, "I just farted super loud 'cept I made the guys think it was Kenny's brother Stan! It was so great! Wanna go get malts at Derby's?"

Benny then asked a pressing question, "Does this mean that the guys on the team will stop hanging me by my boxer shorts now?"

Inevitably, as with everything Peter did, music, eating, school, he played football with passion and excelled. It sucked for us guys because we were now kind of alone on the evil-guy island that most of the other kids were now unwilling to be a part of. Football was big in our town. Sure, kids still called him lard-ass occasionally but it was kind of more in a playful way rather than aimed with malicious intent. It really held no weight anymore, pardon the pun. We were going to have to step up our game especially since Bobby had decided to turn over a new leaf. He had joined the tennis team and started avoiding us guys with his standard blow-off, "my mom and dad grounded me" or "I have tennis practice."

It wasn't entirely shocking but I was pretty let down.

Shortly after Bobby joined the tennis team, he also excelled. And as if that wasn't enough of a blow to us, he began dating Jenny Vestito, the absolute prettiest, most sought after girl in school. She looked exactly like Marsha Brady -- maybe even prettier. Also, you almost never saw her wearing just the standard colorful mini-dress. She almost always had to have on some guy's letterman jacket even if she was indoors and it was 100 degrees. Honestly, Jenny was a moving target --hard to tie down. There was a new guy for every athletic season. Sometimes, she would stay in the relationship for two seasons but not usually.

Peter and Nate hung out as often as they could at the pond even though football practice sometimes made it impossible. On this day Pete premiered a new funky tune – a quirky Jazz piece written for Nate. Nate tapped his feet to the beat. He was even scatting to the music. Pete finished off the tune with a giant laugh. It was a moment they would never forget.

Nate finally expressed his feelings, "So you better protect those fingers, Namath."

Peter laughed, "Yeah. I know. I won't get hurt. Besides, c'mon I'm double the size of most of those guys."

Nate joked, "Yeah. Now we can call you Funkle Footballer!"

By the look on his face, it was obvious Pete didn't like that.

He told Nate, "Nah, music is still my thing, Nate. Funkle Fattie OK, not Funkle Footballer?"

Nate was pleased, "Groovy. You got it Fattie. Praise Jesus! Just testin' ya anyways--"

****

It was a breezy, clear day but the sun was low and the sky was a deep, deep blue. Peter had obviously never been happier. It was disgusting as far as we were concerned. How dare he be happy when we had invested so much time in making him miserable?

On this beautiful, crisp day, he sat in the school-yard with Benny and Sally Anne. Their laughs could be heard yards away.

I approached.

Intending to appear very friendly, I spoke, "Hey guys."

Everyone ignored me except for Sally.

Sally turned to me, "Hey Tommy. How's your grandpa?"

I hung my head low. There was no faking it when it came to this issue.

She knew by the look on my face, "Sorry."

I turned to Peter, "Pete?"

And when he didn't answer, I revved it up, "Pete. PETE!"

Finally he acknowledged me, "Yup."

I asked nicely, "Listen man since you never got to play for

my grandpops, do you think you could?"

He grumbled, "Yeah, sure."

But that wasn't convincing enough for me, "Well, when? 'Cuz it's kinda important? Do y'understand, man? What the hell do you have a healin' sis flute with ya for if you don't use it Fattie?"

There was just no time for "friendly."

Everyone pretty much ignored my rude comments except for Sally.

She snapped at me, "Hey. Watch it, buster!"

Benny could have cared less. He shoved French fries up his nose which kept Peter mostly distracted. I think his super-large nose helped to hold the fries in place. I don't think I've seen a nose that big on a kid, ever. Peter suddenly threw his own french-fries at Benny, as if Benny needed any more props, and they both laughed hysterically.

I was becoming increasingly frustrated. In fact I was furious. I had just about had it. I hurled a can of orange soda in their direction. It exploded but no one got any orange pop on them unfortunately for me because I was aiming specifically for Benny! I lifted my bike which was on its side, kicked up the kick-stand and rode off. But I was far from finished with Fattie...

Sally-Anne finished them off, "God you guys that wasn't very nice. His Grandpa's probably dying. That's what Betty said."

Benny chomped on fries and exclaimed, "Betty? Who the heck is Betty?"

Sally-Anne and Funkle answered in unison:

"My mom"

 "Her mom"

Sally-Anne expounded, "We don't believe in formal titles that suggest power."

Benny answered, very confused, "Huh?"

Funkle came to the rescue. He hit Benny as he rolled his own eyes which basically meant, enough said on this topic.

In response, Benny sneezed out more fries from his nose. Peter cracked up. Now it was Sally's turn to roll her eyes.

Chapter Twenty

It was the last official day of summer, Sept. 20, 1974.
Peter sat by himself at a different area of Salter's Pond than
his usual haunt. He lounged by a rock formation at the edge
of the pond where most of the ducks enjoyed congregating
on a regular basis and collecting bread crumbs. But people
usually avoided this area because of all the duck and Seagull
droppings. Funkle rested his rear-end on a lone grassy patch
with his legs half behind him. As he played his sax, he was
completely alone in the best way, for the first time in a long
while. He looked lost in dreaming and peaceful all at the
same time. It was like he was in some sort of heavenly
repose while he played.

Strewn next to Funkle, at the edge of the pond, were his
cleats, a blue jersey -- which had FUNKLE in white lettering
on the back side and 23 on the front -- and a few books.
Eventually we found out that one of the titles of the books
was, "How to Win Friends and Influence People" by Dale
Carnegie. Funkle honestly needed that book less than any of
us. As far as I was concerned, I figured, give it a year and
he would have been popular enough to run for school
president. He was just starting to have that mass-appeal.
The kind where the nerds aren't exactly threatened by you
and the cool guys must respect you. It's ideal in a high-
school environment. But I wasn't ready to admit that. No
one at the time needed that book more than one Tommy
Greene. But I guess we get lessons when we are ready for
them. Today, indeed you will find a copy prominently placed

on my bookshelf. It reminds me of who I was. Eventually, in the days following the tragedy, I read it at least sixty times.

The pond was unusually free of people that day. The only company Pete had was ducks.

That is until Kenny, Waldo and I began the approach.

I warned the guys, "Look. Just get it and go. Gramps is really hurtin'. You got it?"

Waldo and his awful teeth responded, "Yep. You sure it cures sick guys? 'Cuz that sounds awful dumb to me."

I was not about to be deterred, "Yeah I seen it with my own eyes. Shut up. You're dumb. Dumb-dumb."

Kenny grinned, "It'll be my pleasure to silence that flute playin' sissy. But you owe me Greeney, you hear?"

I always thought that was the stupidest thing a guy could tell you.

And I told him in no uncertain terms, "Yeah. Yeah OK. What do you want a kiss, Kenny? Just get it, OK? And it's a saxello. How many times I gotta tell you, it ain't a flute?"

I really didn't care if they called it a flute. I did the same thing when I made fun of Funkle. I was just generally losing patience with this bunch of punks.

Kenny punched me hard. He didn't have two hands free to *kill* me because he was carrying his new portable radio. I seem to recall that "I Won't Last A Day Without You" by the Carpenters, was playing on the radio when we arrived. So he punched me with his free hand on my shoulder. I felt nothing. My adrenaline was super-charged.

Finally we approached on our collective mission. Peter, still in a musical repose of sorts, was startled.

Kenny placed the radio on the grass and spoke first, "Hey ass-hole give over the fairy flute."

Pete didn't take us seriously as he had been recently experiencing a nice vacation from our torture. I think it made him comfortable and less afraid. But it was an illusion, this false comfort.

Funkle laughed a big belly laugh and spoke, "Nah. Go Away. Shut up. Tommy, you're a creep. I told you that I'd play for your dumb Grandpa! You're such an ugly jerk."

Peter then stood up.

Kenny was steamed, "Blubber-boy, give me that flute, lardo."

I had made sure that Kenny hadn't eaten before the event. I figured, I'd promise him burgers on me because I had saved up my allowance, if he could just help me get the sax. So not only did he hate Peter, but he was extremely hungry.

Kenny attempted to slap the sax out of Peter's hands. Peter instinctively shoved it half way between his waistband and his stomach. He put his fists up in front of his face to protect it like Coach Wilson had said. Kenny took this as an offer to fight.

Pete was out of his league, clearly. Realizing the fist to face action had probably backfired, he picked up a muddy stick to protect himself.

Kenny threw off his jacket and hurled it to the ground. Waldo got behind Pete and held his arms back. Pete clung tightly to his muddy stick. His blue and yellow striped jersey now had huge pit stains.

I hollered in my cracking puberty-affected voice, "Awe shit, Funkle, don't make us fight ya, right, Kenny? This is stupid. Kenny'll kill ya. Just give us the stupid sax. That's what we're here for. Kenny, get it. Grab it! Waldo has his arms, geez! GRAB IT."

But just as I ran over to grab it myself, realizing that I didn't have to wait for Kenny to do it for me, Peter interrupted.

He challenged Kenny, "No. Fight me for it maggot-face. Your brother Stan can't play for shit and you're not worth the duck poop I'm standing on. Must be in the genes--"

Now I knew this was going to get bad. I was just stunned at the bravado with which Funkle spoke. Did he think he was suddenly Ali over night? I mean Kenny and Waldo could still kick his ass.

Kenny spoke maniacally, "Go head, hit me Fattie."

I warned Pete again, "Awe, Funkle, you're a stupid ass! C'mon, geez, just hand it over. We don't wanna hurt ya, do we Kenny? Do we Waldo?"

Pete snickered and spoke louder, "I'm bigger than all of ya. And I ain't afraid no more. C'mon let's go! C'mon Waldo. Is Kenny fightin' your battles for ya ?"

Then for a brief second it seemed that Peter had snapped back into reality out of his brief insane bout of bravado. He had remembered that his valuable sax was still vulnerable. Distracted by thought, he looked down his waist-band to check for it, just for a split second and when he looked back up, Kenny was pointing to his own chin to egg on Peter. But Peter was visibly shaken now as if he had realized the gravity of the moment. Afraid to back down now, he finally swung at Kenny who ducked, causing Pete to swipe at the air. Waldo then went to grab the sax from Funkle's pants but missed. So instead he began kicking Peter so hard with his steel-toe boots. Eventually the sax fell out and down Funkle's pant leg due to the force of the kicks. Peter instinctively bent down to get it and retrieved it with one hand. He already seemed like he was hurting badly from the kicks. The problem is that Kenny also bent down to get it causing the two to accidentally butt heads on the way up.

Peter, so angry from the shock of the head butt, snapped again and went into football-mode. He charged Kenny like it was the beginning of the first quarter. Kenny put his thumbs in his front pockets of his red corduroys as if to say, I am so relaxed. Then he whipped his hair back and laughed. He turned to look at me with a cocky grin, but when he turned back around, Peter had nailed a lucky punch, square on Kenny's jaw.

Waldo narrated as if it was a Madison Square Garden heavyweight championship bout, "That's it blubber boy! Southpaw to the kisser--You're dust now, Fats! You're going down for the count!"

After that first punch, the fight was definitely on. An all-out brawl for blood ensued. Waldo was absolutely killing Funkle. Then before I knew it, there were two new guys who I had never seen or hung out with before who had also jumped in to help Kenny and Waldo kill Funkle. It was now four on one. I was stunned. I just stood there.

Finally, I screamed and urged them to stop, "Kenny, Waldo, guys, STOP! I just want the sax! Jesus Christ! Man, come on. You're gonna kill 'em. He ain't even punching you no more. Hey Pete, just throw me the sax man so we can end this dumb fight. Man, pick it up."

I reached out desperately to grab the sax and got knocked back by someone's punch. I even tried to pull on Funkle's shirt because I figured it would do something, anything. But it didn't work.

Then Kenny socked Peter flat in his nose, hard. There was blood oozing from both nostrils. Peter was clearly in trouble but the guys were deep in this evil frenzy. It was like they had been taken over by wild animals. They weren't even close to stopping. Even the ducks got flustered and flew away.

At a certain point, it turned from a classic young guy's scuffle to a dangerous bar brawl. One of the new thugs, gripped his own stick. He hit Pete on his neck with the stick. Another threw a rock at poor Pete which hit him in his shoulder enough to make Pete's knees buckle.

Then one of the strange guys yelled to Kenny, "Kenny man, you don't even have to pay me for this. I'd beat this lard-ass any day."

It was at that moment that I realized that it was a set-up. Kenny had planned this whole beating and let me think we were going there specifically for the sax. These guys weren't strangers to him. This was all about Kenny getting his rocks off. My grandfather meant nothing to any of my friends. I meant nothing to them. Frightened by the revelation of my friends' true colors, I hid behind a big embankment, screaming, half-to-myself really.

I cried as I looked out and saw Peter really losing a grip on where he was.

I pleaded, "Awe shit! Shit!! Stop! Stop assholes!"

Suddenly, Funkle was pushed dangerously close to the edge of the rock formation. And with one solid punch delivered by Kenny to Pete's big old gut, Funkle or Pete or Skunka-Funka or Chunka-Funka --whatever the nomenclature -- lost his footing, slamming backwards with a big, hard thud onto the rocks, skull first. His precious sax flew into the air and landed only yards from me. As I looked around, paranoid -- because I knew that what I was about to do was wrong on so many levels -- I reached out and quickly snatched the object of my idolatry.

Peter lay like a rag-doll strewn across the pond unconscious. Dark, brownish red blood trickled from his ears. Waldo, unable to resist, lodged one more swift mean kick into Pete's guts, as if to emphasize the fact that Peter was mere trash to him. Kenny, momentarily frozen, actually looked stunned as if the animal that had formerly possessed his spirit had now left and he was alone in the jungle to fend for himself.

Blood soon began to trickle from Funkle's mouth as well. After a few moments, crusty blood collected in his ears and nose.

Suddenly, Kenny yelled, "Tommy, ditch, man. Ditch! Go! We gotta get outta here!"

I ignored him. He didn't wait around.

All my fellow evil-doers had suddenly scattered in many different directions. I burst out from behind the embankment.

Still clutching the sax, completely frozen with fear, I could now hear like a religious chant, Jim Croce sing on the radio, "Bad, Bad Leroy Brown/Baddest man in the whole damn town/Badder than old King Kong/Meaner than a junk-yard dog..." It melded together with the sounds of my own heart-beat which rang like a death knoll in my ears.

Chapter Twenty One

Mrs. F. stormed -- marching like she had been trained in a communist regime -- down the long hospital hallway. The lime green linoleum hospital floors shined with the sheen of a new wax. The nurses trained to maintain calm and unaffected, went about their business as usual. One even joked about her awful date the night before. But a boy's life hung in the balance just across the hall and for one mother, no amount of pristine wax or cool demeanor could diminish that awful reality.

She howled and cried, "Where is he? Where is MY SON?! Where is he? MY SON, GOD DAMN IT! MY SON, take me to Peter, NOW!"

A compassionate nurse responded from her desk, "Ma'am, Ma'am try to stay calm. Are you here for the boy?"

Mrs. F. leaned her body over the nurses' station. With one clean sweep, she swiped away all of the files which caused a paper tornado that eventually collected itself on the green floor.

Mrs. F. was becoming hysterical, "THE BOY … THE BOY? THE BOY'S NAME IS FUNKLE FATTIE! FUNKLE FATTIE THE JAZZ LEGEND! AND HE IS A BEAUTIFUL SAXOPHONE-PLAYING MIRACLE. HE IS NOT "THE BOY." HE IS PETER FUNKLE, MY SON. PETER! WHERE IS HE? WHERE IS PETER?

The nurse wasn't rattled by Mrs. F.'s Behavior.

She answered calmly, "Yes Ma'am, Peter is in Room 005. I will take you to him. But, Mrs. Funkle, I must warn you, it's quite serious...quite serious. I'm so sorry. We are doing everything we can to help your son."

Mrs. F. nodded bravely, acknowledging the reality that faced her. The nurse took her hand and walked to the door of Peter's room - 005. Before entering, Mrs. F paused. She could see through the mini glass window on Peter's door. His head was bandaged and he looked mangled, beaten. The only thing not battered was his eyes. They were closed and you could see the super long length of his thick lashes resting on his cheeks. They made him look cherubic even in tragedy.

Mrs. F. pushed the door open and walked in slowly having left the communist regime back with the shattered remains of her heart at the nurses' station.

Peter lay in his bed, hooked up to machines and swollen. He was completely unresponsive.

Mrs. F. burst out into a wild feral cry, "Oh God Peter what have they done to you?! Why? Why have they done this to you? Why you? Why my son? My good, good soon! You are such a good, good son. I failed you, my sweet boy."

She looked up as we tend to do when asking God for favors.

She groaned, "Oh God, this is all your fault! How...How...How could you let this happen to him, my Peter? What kind of God are you HUH- What kind of evil God are you?"

Ruth entered quietly and stood behind Mrs. F. who was unaware of her presence.

Mrs. F. turned to Peter and cried, "Oh Peter!"

And she held him, "You can't leave me. You've gotta fight! We have cheerleaders to chase and proms to go to and picnics to bob apples at and children to have and weddings and first jobs."

Mrs. F looked again up to the ceiling or God whichever you choose to believe.

She exclaimed, "Oh God please, this is my only baby. Don't do this to me please. Peter c'mon you have music to play. Remember that's God's plan. PETER, PLEASE WAKE UP PLEASE!"

Ruth cleared her throat a little to indicate her presence Mrs. F. turned around and fell into Ruth's arms. They hugged. And they cried and cried and cried.

****

Sun peeked through the small window of Peter's temporary home. The light rested so perfectly on his alabaster skin some of which was now black and blue. Ruth and Mrs. F had slept there. Both lay crooked-necked in chairs next to Pete's bed. Ruth's choice of dress was nothing if not ominous. She wore a black wool sheath dress as if she was already attending his funeral. I never liked her. The dress hem had now creeped up her legs to reveal a white slip underneath. Mrs. F. wore jeans with a Grateful Dead T-shirt and clogs, ever the bad-ass even in crisis. But the picture of Ruth DiBene now juxtaposing Mrs. F in their uncomfortable repose, made me like the cheery secretary even less. I just never liked her.

Suddenly, a doctor entered to interrupt the momentary

slumber. He was tall and lankly with jet black hair and a widow's peak like Eddie Munster. He had no upper lip but a fat bottom lip that jutted out. His white jacket -- which sat over a blue polyester, giant collared, button down shirt patterned with gold airplanes -- had green stitching on the right pocket which read: Dr. Andrasian.

The creak of the door woke both women abruptly. Dr. Andrasian gestured to the two women to join him outside of the room. Groggy, they followed him out to the front desk area.

Clutching Pete's sax, I walked down the long hall slowly. I could see Mrs. F., Mrs. DiBene in funeral-garb and the flamboyant doctor discussing something at the nurses' station. I hunched down to make myself as small as I could. I wanted to fall below the radar of anyone within eye-shot. As I approached the nurses' station, I took a giant deep breath, held it in, and snuck by all three of them into Pete's room. I held onto that sax as if it was my life-line. As soon as I saw Pete, water just began flowing from my eyes in a sheath of tears that no matter how hard I tried to hold, just wouldn't be shut down. My throat hurt so badly from trying to suffocate the big gulp in it that indicated I was crying.

I spoke in a tone just below a whisper, "I didn't mean it Pete. I just wanted you to heal my gramps. You have to wake up and play. I'm sorry you're hurt, truly, but I didn't mean it. Fattie, my gramps is gonna die."

I would do anything to help my grandfather, thus the single-minded rhetoric. I wasn't at all blind to the pain that we had caused Pete, nor the pain that we had caused Mrs. F., I just loved my grandfather that much. Even the fact that I was risking the wrath of Mrs. F. or even the cops, I didn't care. I also don't think I thought for a second that this gentle giant, Funkle Fattie, who was soon becoming so beloved, would actually perish.

In one last ditch effort, I put the sax up to Pete's lips, not fully grasping reality. I was merely at the precipice of manhood, still a boy.

I whispered, "Wake up! Play!! C'mon my Grandpa can't die, Pete. He's all I got. Get better. Play it. C'mon you can hear me, I know you can."

Suddenly Mrs. F. and Ruth walked in finding me in that awkward position with the sax to Pete's lips. My eyes got wider than a guppie and I looked to Mrs. F. in a panic.

She screamed, "YOU! YOU ARE THE REASON MY SON IS LIKE THIS! GET OUT! WHAT ARE YOU DOING HERE! WHAT ARE YOU DOING WITH HIS SAX? GET OUT OF HERE BEFORE I KILL YOU. THIS IS ALL OF YOUR DOING!"

Ruth held her back.

She reminded Mrs. F to keep it together and reminded me to disappear, "Katie, he's a boy. Get out of here, Tommy. You better pray God has mercy on you! Now get out!"

I hated her. She didn't know me at all.

I had to yell back at that old hag, "I didn't touch him, you old bat. I swear! I told them to stop beatin' Pete. I tried to stop them! I just wanted him to play the healing sax for my Grandpa. He's dying, ya know! I swear I didn't touch him,

Mrs. F. I don't want Funkle dead!"

Mrs. F. extended her hand to swing at me, "GET OUT! GET OUT!"

All I could see were Grateful Dead Heads which bounced on her boobs, heading straight toward me.

Ruth pushed me out of the room.

Finally I relented and ran out.

For the next few days, Mrs. F and Ruth sat vigil by Peter's bed. Daily, the "healed" townspeople, the outcast friends of Nate's, filed in one by one, bringing various gifts and laying them next to Peter's bed. Nate was the last to arrive. He stood over Pete and cried. After a few minutes, he reached around the whiskers on his unshaven neck and released the chain with war medals on it. He put it on Peter's chest and while his sun-drenched hand lay there, he looked up to the ceiling...or God...whichever you choose to believe. Mrs. F., watching from the other side of the room now, completely lost it. She looked even less showered than Nate as if that was even possible. The crisis had taken a serious toll on her. Finally, after a few moments, Nate turned to exit. He cupped the back of Mrs. F.'s neck in condolence and left without speaking.

Over the next week, a dark veil threatened to swallow our town whole.

In an effort to combat this dark pall, in the gravity of the black night, a sea of candles illuminated the entire football field to signal hope. Banners lit by candle-light read, "We Love You Funkle!"

All of the "formerly crippled" friends of Peter as well as Sally-Anne, the Lincoln Middle and High School Football Teams, Coach Wilson, the entire Cheer Squad, Carrie the Slut, Benny, Stan, Kenny's jerk-off brother, Lucy and a field of children, held vigil for the boy who didn't even have a name at one point but now was known as Hero to most. Everyone in town came to celebrate the legacy of Funkle Fattie. Many told stories of how he would talk to them in the lunch-room when no one else would. Sick folks spoke of the healing power of his music. Many couples said that after first hearing him play at the fair, they fell in love while listening to the beautiful jazz compositions. Then a children's choir stepped forward.

The chaplain, who was becoming more of a father figure to me, approached the microphone to speak.

He looked up to the sky or the Lord...whichever you choose to believe...and he spoke with deep conviction, "Lord, please watch over your son Peter Funkle, er, ahem, Funkle Fattie. We love him and honor him this night, dear Father. Please heal him as he has done inadvertently for so many souls who have been touched by his music. Please heal him and grant him a speedy recovery."

Carrie cried. Sally-Anne hugged her tightly as she also sobbed. Who would have thought the slut and the syrupy sweet nerd would embrace?

The Lincoln School Children's Choir had a special song prepared for Peter and his family.

The choir, a group smattered with little, snotty-nosed

children and a few cooler girls and guys who were forced to be there by their parents, stepped forward forming a sea of white button down shirts and black trousers or skirts. A sax player who dared to compare to Peter, soloed.

They sang to "Peace in The Valley." The flickering candle-flames swayed in the night.

Everyone was present for this glorious moment in honor of Peter except for me. I smoked as I hid under the bleachers. I was forced to be at the event by the chaplain. But I wouldn't dare come out for fear I would be lynched by the town, although the chaplain had promised me that he wouldn't allow that. I cried as the children sang.

THE FINAL CHAPTER

Mrs. F looked so greasy and worn from the tragedy. At least she was now finally wearing different clothes, a button down, white men's shirt and carpenter pants. She stepped out of Pete's room momentarily. I watched her leave. Dressed in a long, black pea coat and red and white striped bell-bottom pants, I ran in adjusting my gait when the rubber from my sneaker soles let out a squeak. I walked over to Pete's bed, some of his bruising and swelling had gone now. I lifted up the saxophone sitting on the bed-stand that I had left there in exchange for my life. I sat over Peter and I tried to play it myself. I hate to admit this, but I had lost hope now that Pete would ever recover. So I had devised a new plan.

My thought was, if the saxophone had healing benefits, which I believed it did, then the source of the playing was inconsequential. All that was needed was a new player and a healing intention. After much thought, I decided this had to be me. I put the mouth piece up to my lips. The first notes, I warbled terribly. After a few moments, I was able to master a couple of basic sounds. My imagination ran away with me. For a second I thought I could actually envision a glimmer of hope for my grandfather. After Peter's hospitalization, any hope I did have had vanished. I felt a wash of relief come over me. I put the golden sax under my coat and snuck back out avoiding anyone's line of sight.

Out of breath, I arrived at my Gramp's bedside with the magical sax in hand. There were no obstacles present for the first time in a long time. The chaplain and the nurse were otherwise distracted as they enjoyed tea and deep conversation. I could play and heal without interruption. I pulled Gramps' door closed leaving a little room to see if anyone was coming. I sat by my Gramps and began to play what little I had learned, albeit the same notes repetitively. Gramps looked dead. I leaned in to see if I could hear him breathe. I was startled to hear a shallow raspy, anguished rattle.

I pleaded, "Gramps, listen. This is it. This is it. It will heal you. Just hang on."

But once again within seconds, the pesky chaplain was there to foil my plans.

He spoke in a metered pattern. "Son...come out here. I need to talk to you."

I looked down at the saxello as I followed him out. I was caught in a very big way. He knew this wasn't mine.

He continued, "Kenny and the other boys are in big trouble. Did you have anything to do with it, with the beating? And son, while you are standing there holding Peter Funkle's sax, I would think very carefully about lying to me. The Lord sees everything. You hear me, boy?"

My knees trembled, "Nah. Nothing-- I tried to stop 'em. I swear! I didn't touch Pete. D'you b'lieve me; You b'lieve me right? I ain't lying. I only took the sax to heal Gramps. It heals even though youse don't b'lieve nothin' I say."

The nurse and the chaplain shook their heads as if they were disturbed by my words. I ran back defiantly and played some more for Gramps.

Through my salty tears, I begged, "C'mon, Granpy, listen. I know it works. I've seen it work. Wake up! Wake up!"

He didn't wake and suddenly I felt the chaplain's knuckles digging into my neck as he grabbed me by the collar to lift me out. I kneed him in the shins and ran with the sax in my hand, all the way to the pond.

It was unusually warm out on this first day in October. I sat by the rock quarry where only the ducks went. I sat on duck droppings that stained my red cords, desperately trying to teach myself to play. Suddenly I felt creepy. I looked up to see Nate's eyes on me. But by now, I was in such a dark place that I figured, if he was going to take me down for my actions, so be it. I didn't care about anyone anymore because none of it seemed to matter without my grandfather. And I couldn't understand in my little brain at the time, why no one seemed to understand that I was losing my only parent. My actions, while shameful, were a desperate cry for help. I guess I had formed such a reputation that it superseded my needs as a young child or maybe they just plain didn't care. I was angry about it though.

Hours elapsed. I played while a furious Nate watched without incident. His eyes never left me. Finally getting somewhere, I was able to eke out actual children's songs fairly well. When I tired, Nate approached.

He spoke, the smell of whiskey on his breath, pungent, "Y'know boy, sometimes it's not about the shell but instead

it's about the spirit inside the shell. Like, take that old sax.
It doesn't look like much, hell you boys even called it a flute,
a fairy flute if I remember right. But when it's mixed up with
the right spirit, look what it done. Kinda like Fattie huh? His
shell is all big and lumpy but look how he moved this whole
damn town. And look what your spirit did. Your shell didn't
matter much did it? When you stood by and did not a damn
lick a'nuthin' to help that boy? The spirit mixed up inside you
was just pure bad at that moment, wasn't it?"

I whispered, lowering my eyes down to the ground because
looking up to God wasn't working, "I guess. But you don't
know nothin' about my spirit, hear me? I just wanted my
Gramps to live. Don't that count; Don't it? I don't got no
one, Crazy Nate! Don't you bastards get nothin' I been
sayin' this whole time?!!"

I peeled off as fast as I could, sax gripped tight at my side.

Nate stood there watching me leave for a moment. For a
split second I kind of liked the guy. He actually listened and
he didn't beat the crap out of me.

Nate lit a cigarette and walked for a ways until he finally
came upon his wheelchair which was sitting under an old
tree. It was draped with an old army bag hanging off the
back of the seat. He grimaced as he yanked the bag off the
chair handle and placed it on the ground. After looking at
the chair for a moment as if expecting it to answer him or
impart wisdom, he kicked it until it rolled. When it didn't
move far enough, he kicked the wheelchair so that it made a
zig-zag journey until it finally landed in the pond. In a much

needed moment of release, Nate broke down from the heavy weight of the grief.

****

My grandpa hung on by a very fragile thread. I would make one last attempt to wake Peter. As I approached Pete's door, I lowered my body and creaked it open to see if the coast was clear. It was so I entered the room.

I knelt by his bedside, glancing occasionally for the arrival of Ruth or Mrs. Funkle.

I gently put the sax up to Peter's mouth and begged again for him to wake up and play. After a few moments, all despair had settled in. I knew my grandpa had only days left anyway, maybe even minutes. My boyhood faith, my unwavering belief that I could change the course of nature, had faded now into the kind of conditional acceptance that we all unfortunately learn as we reach adulthood. I had given up. The faith that I had so clung to despite all of the warnings, had finally given way to reality. Peter was nearly gone and my grandpa would soon be gone as well.

Then for a second, I think a tiny residue of my innocence fought back. I put the sax up to my lips and played for Pete. My last micro-ounce of faith allowed me to believe in a last-minute miracle that might include Peter or Gramps or both. I played so badly but paused only to speak what was sitting on my heart like a block of concrete.

I said finally and with the humblest of intentions, "Wake up, buddy. You can do it. Please wake up. It doesn't heal when I play it for Gramps. It was you. It was you. I'm so sorry. I DIDN'T MEAN FOR THIS TO HAPPEN, PLEASE! I know you think I did but I just thought you were a healer. Just as you got your mom, Mrs. F., Gramps is all I got. D'ya see? I ain't got nothin' against you Pete really man. I even thought maybe we'd be friends for real when Kenny and them guys got outta the picture, least I thought about it anyway. The whole town's prayin' for ya, buddy. More than I got. You deserve it, Funkle. You been so good and I ain't been nothin' but rotten. But I got no one prayin' for my Gramps 'cept me. You and your sax is my last hope, see. Please Pete. I'm sorry. Please wake up. I'll never call you nothin' bad again and I swear I'll kill those monkeys if they ever try to hurt ya again. I owe it to ya buddy."

And with that, I waited a minute for any response. A sneeze, an eye-twitch, any glimmer of hope. Nothing happened. My frustration eventually took over. I realized it was never going to work. In anger, I threw the sax down onto the bed. It seemed to bounce almost in slow motion as I exited. That was the last I saw of it...and Funkle.

In that split second somewhere between throwing down that old sax and its eventual landing onto the bed, I left my boyhood behind in Pete's hospital room. Any last ounce of innocence had faded into oblivion.

As I began the long journey down the hospital corridor the green linoleum floor met my feet, smacking hard at my every step, preparing me for my transition to adulthood.

My Grandpa died that night.

I could have predicted Gramps' death to the minute. I had

felt the impending event in my gut as I walked toward the end of the hospital hall. As soon as I saw the exit doors, I saw Ruth and Mrs. F. entering. Panicked about something related to Peter, they ran past me frantically toward his room which was in the opposite direction. My stomach plummeted as I assumed that this was probably related to Funkle's impending passing.

****

Mrs. F. hurled herself onto Pete's bed-side. The nurses were frantically crying and making the sign of the cross. The sax that I had played in earnest desperation moments earlier to wake him, rested right by Peter's chest, still fresh with my spit on the mouth-piece.

   Peter wiggled a finger. He wiggled another.

****

I walked through the first set of hospital doors. They swung closed behind me as I made my way to the reality of the outside world. I flung open the second set of doors...
...Peter's eyes flew wide open as if he was forced awake.

   His blue saucer-like irises revealed that he indeed recognized his mother.

   Ruth screamed, "Pete's healed!"

****

   I moved in with the chaplain. He moved us to Boston where I attended prestigious Catholic schools and left my bully persona behind me. We never spoke of Peter again. I've gone on to lead quite an exciting, fulfilled life. Although, the first couple of months after we left Ipswich were truly a living hell, I learned to adjust ... and speak proper English. The four other guys Kenny, Waldo, and the two unnamed strangers, who I soon found out were named, Louis and Jason, were all sent away to various delinquent boys' homes. I'm sure the chaplain made some sort of deal to keep me out of a boys' home which ultimately, I am certain, saved my life. I only read in the paper of the musical prodigy boy in Ipswich who woke up miraculously from death's door. By that point, he no longer even had a name. It was like he became a enigmatic symbol for so much more.

Ironically in my search to find healing, I became a healer. Karma doesn't always work the way you think. I feel like my obligation and passion as a healer is the work I must do to complete a debt owed. Today, I think about Fattie often. Although I don't know where he went, he disappeared. Many times, I have searched on Google and Facebook and nothing, not even the name "Funkle" exists. But I am sure wherever he lives now, he is changing his little corner of the world, one note at a time. I accept that as a hard and fast truth. That's all I need.

****

My cries echoed through the hollow hospital corridor that day. I was unaware that the world as I knew would soon change permanently. Nor was I aware that Funkle Fattie had returned.

The story goes that as Peter's eyes flew wide open and he smiled at Mrs. F., the hospital volunteer choir could be heard singing, "Peace in the Valley."

Others said there was no choir that day. Those folks swear to this day that it was the angels.

EPILOGUE

A man walks slowly and confidently down the hospital corridor, smacking his loafers on the green linoleum. His red hair thinning with age, he wears a white lab coat that hangs over his beige suit jacket sleeve as he carries it out at the end of a long day. He approaches the exit. A young blonde nurse crosses his path, hurriedly.

She sweetly greets him, "Have a good night, Dr. Greene."

Without stopping, he responds, "Thank you. I plan on it. I'm going to a concert this evening. I need some healing music if you know what I mean. Some beautiful Jazz harmonies, like medicine for the soul."

She laughs and notes, "I heard that. Have a great night, Dr. Greene."

He smiles, "As I do every day, Fran. This night is no different. I am more than blessed. Have a good night, Fran."

She coos, "Thank you, Doctor."

Dr. Greene opens the swinging hospital doors that lead to the outside and walks out to the parking lot. He spots his car, a black BMW 340i. His beautiful wife sits in the passenger seat obviously having moved so he may take the driver's seat. Her long, black, silky hair can be seen flowing over her shoulder. She winks at him with her gorgeous, doe eyes and then sticks her arm out of the window, her wrist adorned with a diamond encrusted Rolex. She waves happily at the sight of her husband.

Dr. Greene hurries to greet his family. He approaches the shiny auto, opens the door and sits in the driver's seat.

He looks back and exclaims, "Hi there, Rattigan. Ready for to hear some wonderful music?"

An over-weight boy of about ten years old, with a mane that is a flaming burnt red color, leans up toward the driver's side, smiling at his dad. Then he pats him on the back.

The boy, wise beyond his years, remarks while impersonating an evangelist in the pulpit, "Praise Jesus, Dad! Praise Jesus, I said."

Then as he looks up toward the ceiling of the BMW, he hollers, "Let the healing begin! Music for the soul right Dad-- Music for the soul--"

Dr. Greene answers, amused, "Yes son. Music for the soul, indeed it is. Music for the soul--"

The car drives away slowly. It leaves the hospital in its rear view. It passes Fred Derby's, making its way along winding roads. It passes an old gas station where a wheelchair bound Vet can be seen pan-handling. His sign reads: **Gulf War Vet Will wAsh YoUR WindoWs for food**.

The shiny car continues on its path, Rattigan's tiny freckled nose pressed against the back-seat window. It passes the Lincoln Middle School, past the old railroad tracks and past the football field where cheerleaders are practicing, and finally past an old dilapidated sign which reads, Salter's Pond. The luxury car disappears into the dusk along with the long ago pain of a young Tom Greene.

The doctor retires the memory of Funkle Fattie for tonight. It will reemerge as it always does. But just as he drives away, somewhere deep inside the edges of the pond, someone else is retelling the story of Funkle Fattie to all who will listen. Maybe another former bully recounts now the tale of a young boy who refused to have his spirit muffled by hate. And yet another passes on the details of a young, courageous musical prodigy who forever changed his little corner of the world in Ipswich, Massachusetts during the summer of 1974.

And as the wind whistles through the trees that cover and protect Salter's Pond, if you listen really well, you may hear the sound of healing music.

Made in the USA
Lexington, KY
05 July 2013